Memories need good markers.

It might be the smell of Old Spice near a shaving mirror, or patchouli in an autumn garden. What things bring us back to the innocence and safety of our grandma or grandpa's sweet embrace?

What might spark a recollection of a time when we were united in the Garden of Eden, or a single voice, working to build the great tower of Babel on the continent of Pangea?

Within these pages we find that thread.
Ole factory senses re-ignite as we follow Hubudi on its journey through time and space, re-membering everything piece by piece.

Union is our history.
Union is our destiny.
Remember…

Jay Horne's

A Novel of Rootworld

PRESENTED BY BOOKFLURRY INC.

Jay M. Horne, Cover Artist and Illustrator assisted by Dall-e

Cataloguing Publication Data

Horne, Jay M., 1980-

Hubudi / Jay M. Horne

ISBN: 979-8-9913831-0-3

Library of Congress Control Number: 2024917466

Bookflurry Inc.

Bradenton, FL

for Mom
… and those who inspire to dream.

Also, for Angela.

Gifts and their meanings. Stories can change. Sometimes for the better. Sometimes, because those who tell them remember with more clarity—and love.

Table of Contents

HUBUDI

INTRODUCTION: THE DOLMEN

A hand trembles as it works a key in an ancient padlock. The hand is mine and it turns with surprising ease. The chain coils to the ground like a sleeping serpent and the gate creaks open just enough for me to squeeze through sideways.

They say Father Time can see anything in the viewing lens of his magiscope. Like Santa Clause, watching when you're sleeping, knowing when you're awake. I never really believed any of that mess, but now that Dad's gone, I wonder. Could he see me now, from wherever he is? I hope not.

I shuffle forward toward the stone monolith, weathered soles scuffing the earthen path. What did that placard say? The words echo in my mind as I approach the dolmen:

Who but I can know the secrets of the unhewn dolmen?

Who but I can reveal the mysteries of the moon?

Who but I can find the secret resting place of the sun?

The structure glimmers like a mirage under dappled twilight creating shifting patterns across the ancient stone. I glance down at my feet, at these unfamiliar sandals caked with jungle mud. My Pumas are gone. My wallet too. The fine trench coat I remember wearing in London has been replaced by this worn Clyde and Foster hoodie.

"Who but I," I say, pushing further into the clearing, "would wake up in a jungle, unable to remember how I got here?"

The dolmen stands before me, its secrets hidden behind an impenetrable veil of stone.

"Who but I?"

HuBudi

PROLOGUE

Father Time watches as the scene takes to the wind, adjusting the focus on his magiscope with his remote, an automagic response of someone who's been channel-surfing through eternity. He takes a swig from an ancient mug that reads "World's #1 Dad" and chuckles softly to himself.

"Kid's got no idea what he's walking into," he mutters, watching the man at the dolmen gate. The crystal sphere is cradled between two golden dragons and inside, the image turns then climbs, up and up, dodging tendrils of leaf.

Father Time had designed this whole cosmic show once, back before he'd forgotten the script. Now he lived it day by day like everyone else, though he had the advantage of better seats and instant replay. This magiscope never quite worked the way you wanted it to.

The vision in his magiscope circles upward, away from the man who wonders at the gate. Moss swaying, boughs bending, with Mother's grace. Finally breaching the canopy of the living forest and still, up it goes until the view becomes that of a whole planet with the many continents of Earth. The tip of the once great pyramid of Babel, now called Giza, standing as a mere point above the sands—a tiny fraction of its true grandeur buried beneath, cast down in an age long past.

"Yeah, yeah," Father Time says, fast-forwarding through some of the more tedious geological epochs. "Note to self: next round,

maybe don't give humans quite so much ambition right out of the gate."

Father Time had been there. Father Time had been everywhere. The magiscope only helps better organize the memories of it all, like an interactive photo album of sorts—though he sometimes wondered if he was remembering things right, or just making it up as he went along. Hard to tell the difference when you're living your own forgotten masterpiece.

The image inside transitions with the blue of the sky and shifts from this future scene, taking him back to the beginning. He sees only water in the transparent sphere. A water that begins to turn, and then swirl in torrents. Then, in the white foam of chaos, there is a spark that only Father Time would describe as hydrogen and oxygen creating heat. Others might call it the will of God.

"Well, can't blame them for not knowing about molecular chemistry," Father Time shrugs.

Then a geyser erupts, filling the outer shell of the scope with steam. Soon, lava is spewing forth. Atmosphere forming, and liquid obsidian cooling to become stone. A great landmass appears, and a people imbued with the very same elements, coming forth from their own mother's wombs. Their blood the water, bodies, the cool earth, their breath, steam on the air, and their thoughts, the very fiery spark of imagination!

A great pyramid stands at the center of the great mass of land and Father Time grunts when he sees his hand cast it down. It always has that effect on him—a mixture of regret and necessity, like grounding your teenager for their own good. Humanity was not ready. Their unity and wonder came not from awe but from want. The tower was buried, the languages scattered, the continents divided.

"Harsh but fair," he muses, though his expression suggests he's still not entirely convinced he made the right call. "Sometimes being the responsible parent sucks."

The magiscope's view ripples, shifting to the present where crowds of people from different races and continents gather around Giza in awe. Father Time thrums his fingers on the arm of his chair, a gesture both ancient and oddly modern. In markets and plazas across the world, ancient enemies break bread together.

He leans forward, suddenly interested. "Well, I'll be..."

Perhaps, at last, they are ready.

The magiscope's image drops low, finally settling on a tavern in London, where the man that had been at the dolmen sits, drinking a beer, bound for memory loss.

Father Time raises his mug in a toast to the screen. "Here's to forgetting the plan so you can live the surprise, kid. Trust me, I know how that feels."

Then, the God thinks to himself, "Yes."

"Giza... will... rise."

I. LONDON 2030

It was unusual weather for an October night when I could no longer deny that my self-medicating was aggravating my hereditary misfortunes.

The smoke from half a dozen cigarettes hung in the tavern like London's infamous fog beneath the yellowed ceiling.

“Tapping out, Jesse?” the bartender asked, slinging his dishrag over his shoulder. He eyed the bills on the counter and I nodded. “Cold out there tonight,” he began but I put a hand up.

The man was collecting the money but looked over his shoulder when I’d silenced him. On the flatscreen above the bar, a clinical-looking woman in a white coat gestured to brain scans.

"Antihistamines and alcohol; two major contributors to the onset of early Alzheimer's—accelerating neurodegeneration by up to forty percent in predisposed individuals."

Great. I'd been drowning my father's diagnosis—and now my own—in both substances for years. The memory of his vacant eyes in that nursing home flashed painfully. I looked down into my Guinness. I might be joining him sooner than I thought?

I drained the remainder of my pint and squeezed past two broad-shouldered men arguing about football. Outside, Paddington's streets glistened with fresh snow under Victorian lamplights. The bitter cold brought a clarity I both craved and feared.

A couple approached—young, oblivious, laughing. Their eyes met mine for a second before darting away. Something about my expression must have alarmed them. Or perhaps they glimpsed the shadow of what I was becoming—a man steadily forgetting himself.

Who could blame them? What had I come to London for? Something about dragon bones and an ancient monument? The details jump away like a water snake.

They were gonna look away regardless. In the end, I just pull the neck of my trench coat tight as the faces pass, then stare out at the yellow glow of the upstairs windows of the old Brunswick Inn.

Then, it's right back to all-encompassing thoughts about time, and how much of it I really have left to spend. Because that's what being alive really is, right? The ability to think, to remember.

I stop at the entrance of the hotel and unscrew the cap of the little bottle of cough syrup. Antihistamines. Take a swig anyway.

The door to the Brunswick was heavy against the wind. One's always bolted to the floor, and it's always the one I try first. This time's an exception. There's something; I'd remembered which.

Maybe I *was* alive.

II. THE BRUNSWICK INN

Immediate warmth, accompanied by a few falling flakes that blew in and disappeared on the tile floor. Like closing the airlock on a spaceship.

Back in the States, my father used to throw his coat on a rack similar to the one standing at the entrance to the lobby. I remember some things from boyhood, just not everything. Memories hurt. Maybe because they're so good.

The inside of the Brunswick, in a way, reminds me of home. The owner lets his son Jimmy run things here. Nice enough lad. Rosy cheeked, big smile, greased hair like the teens do. Not your commercial inn. Family owned. Perhaps it's why I'll remain for the week.

Or maybe it's her. There she is again, sitting on the leather easy chair smoking her cigarette in the lobby. Looking my way.

The door got her attention. Nothing like a door slammed in the wind and a trench coat settling from the snow. Cool.

But she's cool, too. She's not alarmed, just curious.

I hook my flat cap on the rack.

She blows a thin line of smoke.

"Welcome back, Mr. Bankole!" cries Jimmy from the desk. "Mind the tile."

I do my best to keep the snow off the landing. Doubling the duster over my arm and tossing it over the back of the loveseat by the coffee table.

Her legs are crossed in a way that the slit in her dress eventually becomes part of the cushion. The rest is legs.

She has me now. I'm settling into the loveseat and we've seen each other. Not to say something would be awkward.

There are crisps on the coffee table. A copper ashtray sits under the stained-glass lamp by her side.

I opt for the little biscuit. *Crunch.*

I tell myself, 'Enjoy beauty, but do not seek to possess it for possession's sake alone.' Another one of those memories.

I settle. Chew.

She watches.

Chew some more.

"Every night," she says wistfully.

Olive eyes. Lips like a guava. Hair long and straight. Dark, like someone lifted the contrast too far.

I stop chewing. Swallow. And then it begins...

She leans forward, her eyes locked on mine. "You've been drinking," she says, another tug off the cigarette, and she flicks the ash over her left shoulder. The large flake lands expertly in the copper tin. My eyes follow it through the whole motion.

"I'm just back from the bar," I reply, cautiously.

She nods smartly through my response, eyebrows raised, eyes ushering me through accusingly. A placid stare reminds me of Elvira, or Morticia Addams, characters I may have seen on late-night television.

"Again?" she asks, and before I can develop a rebuttal, she continues, "You know what they say about doing the same thing over and over again?"

Jimmy has wandered over and starts wiping the coffee table. When I acknowledge him, the young man offers an empathetic smirk. Non-intrusive, yet a look shared by gentlemen courting women for generations.

Really, it's an unexpected stroke of luck. Another gentle male presence stirs me into engaging the lady's wit rather than succumbing to the sourness her poorly timed, yet playful accusation had stirred inside.

Sarcasm then. “The insane expect to change,” I say. “I have no such delusions."

Not bad, says Jimmy's expression before he escapes the awkward exchange.

She's preparing another thoughtful drag.

"And you?" I ask tactfully, aiming at her own bad habit.

The cigarette stops an inch from her lips, smoldering. Her eyes still watch the smoke cascade from the tip. But then they twitch my way and connect as her mouth parts in a pleased smile of white teeth.

"Touché."

Now, I watch her as she allows herself the pleasure. Her eyes never leave mine while she inhales through pursed pink lips.

I could tell her everything.

Then she exhales again, still staring, but tucking her chin and leaning even further into the chair. Her top leg is capped with a high-heel hanging loose from her toes, which she's flexing and making the shoe do a little dance. On, off, on, off.

We share a little silence as Jimmy straightens the coats, secretly eavesdropping, as people naturally do.

I think of reaching for another crisp and continuing with my confident banter but stop. A premonition of the line of questioning stings me. Such terrible questions. Is there life without memory? Can you live without memories? Can you do without previous experience? What about when mine gets really bad?

You don't ask strangers questions that big, so I get a little lost in my own head.

She sees the drawback in my eyes. Deep, lively blue, suddenly still.

She knows that look. She once loved a look like that.

"So, what's the culprit?" Her question is a way of staunching off the flow of her own memories.

I'm back, but not fully. Not complete enough for the full truth to come out.

I shake my head. "Nothing. You know, just biding time."

"Time for?"

A little circle with her smoking hand. Another eyebrow raise. More accusations.

I take everything personally when I'm in a bad mood. She doesn't notice.

"The ferry."

Finally, we exchange names. Evelyn. Then the first handshake.

The copper bolt, holding the wrong door, breaks off in its catch as the two ruffians from the bar stumble in.

Old friends.

Problem with friends is: everything's a joke. And the bigger one is oblivious to Jimmy trying to help, now that he's seen Evelyn. *Already taken, Asshole.*

I think it while following his blatant stare.

I was just getting in the mood for jokes. Maybe for the first time in a while. Now I'll have to get serious.

Here we go again. Every time a good thing comes, its opposite follows. As if God says, "You like her? Well here's your chance to prove it." Okay then, I think, wanting to revolt, but losing patience with my stubbornness instead. I mentally reach for the switch of my internal electromagnet, changing polarities, powering up.

Yeah, Jimmy, they're perfectly capable of taking care of their own coats.

One snatches the dishrag from Jimmy's shoulder and uses it like a whip. The other laughs. Then his eyes again. Staring at her.

Here... we... go...

"Are you coming?" Evelyn asks.

She's standing. Has crushed the butt into the little copper tray. I glance at it. It's warped and sooty.

But her eyes get me under direction again.

I follow those emeralds to infinity and see the wooden steps heading up into the loft. Smoke draws in on itself therc. It's where my room is.

Coming? Funny word. Not yet. Maybe I'm still in the mood for jokes.

Then, I'm on my feet too, and the sound of her stilettos on the stairs is all that's left for the two troublemakers to fantasize about.

She has saved me from one of those self-depreciating choices that I hate.

Maybe I could live without memories. But that would mean someone eventually making all these choices for me.

Who could care that much? I think of my father.

III. EVELYN'S TALE

Evelyn does a one-eighty at the top of the steps and begins carefully cross-stepping her way down the violet and gold carpet of the hall.

She clutches her scarf to her with her right hand while her left does a little guesswork as to which room is mine.

Two steps back, then a little pirouette, and she uncertainly points to door number three, watching my expression for clues. I give a tight smile but rock my head back and forth, my eyes holding her stare.

It takes her two more playful attempts, but she stays with the rooms on the right for the win.

Out of the twelve possible doors on the upper floor of the Brunswick Inn, it's not a bad score.

She knows she's picked correctly when I start fishing for the key.

"Ah hah. Lucky seven. I should have known," she says.

The brass catch clicks. The electric door-side candelabra gutters when I twist the handle. Filaments in each orange curly bulb protest against time. Or maybe it's the wiring.

I open it for her but, before following her in, take one last look down to the end of the hall. There's a marked absence of merry giggling in that direction. Now, only the familiar solitary vase of carnations stands in silence before the window.

Most the rooms at the Brunswick are laid out uniformly. However, the furniture in my room is oddly tiny.

Evelyn easily navigates between the ornate bedpost and the small coffee table. Then, after a pause, she goes to take her seat in one of the little chairs, embarrassed at trying to look proper in such a cramped space.

I toss my coat onto the pinstriped quilt and turn my attention to the mini fridge, offering her some privacy in the struggle.

"Scotch?" I ask over my shoulder, rummaging for the tumbler.

"Please."

When I produce the Johnny Walker, she's in place. Fit into the small chair like a kindergartner at snack time. Cute.

The tumbler slides onto the table. Two ice cubes ring in the bottom of the glass, dropped from little aluminum tongs. The little jingle makes her eyes draw back.

Jewels, looking up at me. White saucers on a caramel sea.

What do I see in them?

Later, I would know the tinkling sound brought a memory of her father's stories of Christmas snow. Snow that was falling here, in early October.

Who'd have thought?

She wraps her hand around the cool glass. Tilts it to let the ice slide back and forth.

"Only one?"

I spin the tin top off the scotch bottle with a flick of my thumb, and then it's in my right-hand grip. Like a magician or an overconfident maître d'.

"Guess we'll have to share," I say, spreading my arms. Then pour her scotch. "Really, I've had plenty."

The scene is set. Ice cracking in the liquid heat. During two pours, Evelyn tells me she'd never have known the experience of snow if she hadn't left home.

Father Time adjusts the magiscope's focus as Mother Earth settles into her own easy chair beside him, a steaming cup of cocoa warming her hands.

The scene flips from Evelyn's face to Jesse's inside the orb.

I tell her a little about my father's early Alzheimer's, my own diagnosis, and the disturbing news I've just heard, she gets a better picture of me.

What is it she pictures? Well, my father once told me that there are three things a man is. What he thinks he is, what others think he is, and what he really is. I'm certain that all three are ambiguous. Deep down, maybe I'm trying to find an identity. The problem is, the idea is so threatening to me that I won't let it surface. I tell her of my interest in legends. The mantle of Arthur; fabled to hide the bones of a dragon. I'd read about it as a boy.

"I don't think I'll actually see the bones! I just want to visit the spot. According to myth, there's charms that activates the cloak. So, unless there's been a significant magical discovery, I will be enjoying a peculiarly shaped pile of stones. The ferry takes you out to the lighthouse. It's on the furthest needle." A silly boy's adventure, I think, once it's out.

"No," she says. "If we give up on magic. What hope do we have?"

I think she may be feigning interest so almost don't comment but finally say, "Well, the Jehovah's witnesses have been holding out in their own special way."

She smiles and I wonder if religion is really as dangerous a topic as politics. "I don't think it's Jesus they're waiting for." She pronounces Jesus in Spanish so it comes out Hazeus. "I think they just miss the miracles."

Father Time pauses mid-sip of his beer, the magiscope's image lingering on Evelyn's face.

"Did you hear that?" Mother Earth blurts out, leaning forward in her chair.

"What? Of course they miss the miracles," Father Time says about to pause it.

"No, silly! They said his name."

A fond smile crossed Father Time's features. "Been a while since anyone said his name like that."

"Our boy," Mother Earth sighs, her hand reaching across the side table and finding Father Time's. "Always did love making an entrance."

"Yeah, well, he gets that from you," Father Time chuckles. "The dramatic flair, anyway."

The two settled back, watching together in their chairs, as Jesse continued.

Feeling a little foolish for revealing my strange interest, I simply nod, then ask, "So, when did you leave home?"

Luckily, she went with it. "It was about nine years ago; totally against my parents' wishes."

"The bird's gotta leave the nest at some point," I say.

"Well," she says, relaxing back as best she can in the little chair. "I can't say it wasn't selfish."

The stoic look she gives me then almost dares me to keep defending her decision.

She says that she can still remember the sandy floors of their adobe home, dug into the side of a jagged mound of clay. That the fires littering the town at night still shine in her mind. The wisps of smoke, and the sound of the whip-poor-wills cooing. The canopy of the rainforest sometimes opening overhead to dry the earth where her mother was a master gardener. All still vivid to her.

She recalls to me watching as her mother turned the soil along the moist edge of the forest because that was where the best peppers would grow. The outskirts of the village having been alive with colors year-round. Fruits and vegetables of every variety forming a sanctuary there. She says that the villagers loved to be among the harvest whether working or not.

When my silence holds, she continues.

"It was a reap and sow existence. Give and get. I still try to practice it. What we do for the Earth, she does for us, Father used to say; for we are truly one.

"Understand, I was never meant to 'leave the nest,' so to speak. I was next in line. Not only had my father educated me with his stories, but my mother in medicines." She paused briefly then said, "And her experiences in flight."

Evelyn's fingers trace an invisible pattern on the arm of her chair, the movement precise, ritualistic. My eyebrows raise.

"Our tribe, Oxychana, derived its name from an herb. We used it to encourage our mystical states. Special quids made from a family of sage brush. Its petals were the bluest hue, but the power was in its root, which elders ground and rolled in the leaf. We packed these quids in between our gums and teeth, and the juice would go to work. Visions."

She pauses, studying my reaction. I try to keep my face neutral, but something must show—curiosity, perhaps disbelief—because she leans forward, her eyes suddenly intense. "Do you really believe in magic?"

"You saw me with the scotch, didn't you?" I knew it was a weak argument.

"You know what I mean. Beyond parlor tricks."

I let a silence linger as I thought of Merlin, Arthur's magician. He had been a major character in the legend, but I really couldn't say anything toward his magic. "Yes," I said finally. I couldn't have her thinking I had no hope, after all.

"You think I speak of simple hallucinations? No. The Oxychana leaf was supposed to show truths. Past and future would merge. Glimpses of when the continents were one, before the world was broken apart."

I was rapt. Mentally associating her story to the isle of Avalon before it was lost to the mists.

"Mother was Chieftain when it came to such things. They called her The Moon. She and I would take these spirit flights together. Naturally, as a youth, the visions were incredibly immersive. The great tower before it was cast down. How could a child forget such things?"

She pauses briefly and lets me digest. I pour her a third round.

"Thank you," she says. "I believed it—in magic, most of my life. The Sun, The Moon, and The Earth in perfect harmony? It was convincing. A union supposed to bring revolution for our tribe; revitalize it. Only because it was already falling to segregation from the onrush of modern age. But, I can't feel guilty about abandoning the cause. All of those who came before were unsuccessful..."

Evelyn hears a familiar sound come through the walls as she goes for the last vein of liquid amber.

Light female laughter from room twelve.

Her eyes are glued to their corners, listening more than looking. I notice. When she looks back, I'm blushing.

"So you hear them, too?" she asks, accusingly. I reach for the glass, now empty, and she covers it with her palm, smiling. "Don't deny it."

Her look says she's had enough to drink for now.

"I hear them," I say, "just not sure whether to be depressed about it or not."

She laughs at my sarcasm. "Try staying next door."

I give up on the tumbler and stow the scotch instead. "Ah, a bit jealous, huh?"

"Of three ladies, laughing... making love?" Now, she's trying to keep her knees together while she takes her feet. "Pfft. Not so jealous as to get depressed about it."

I smile and go to assist her. She's clearly wobbly.

"Thanks," she says as I help steady her.

Her eyes are on mine. My eyes are losing the battle to refrain from the high hem of her dress. She doesn't mind.

Evelyn produces her cigarettes from a pocket under her left arm. "Do you think the lobby is safe?"

"I haven't heard anything for a while. We can always hope."

"I must say the couch there is much more comfortable."

"Worth the risk then? If only Gerald served scotch," I say as she makes her way, more composed. She lifts a palm to me in a gesture of enough while she opens the door.

"Right behind you," I say, then rummage in my bedstand. "Just going to get my pipe."

The door clicks behind her, and I move swiftly to pull out a pen and pad and start jotting notes. The shape of the silver moon pendant I'd glimpsed at her throat, the exact color of her eyes, the words she'd used—Oxychana, The Moon, The Sun.

Something about it all feels familiar. Something I can't afford to forget.

IV. SIMPLE PLEASURES

Evelyn is tucked into the corner of the red sofa, a white cigarette between her first and second fingers, her other elbow resting on the arm. I see that the spaghetti strap on her supporting side has fallen to her bicep.

I notice these things from beside the check-in counter where Gerald is now working.

No need to assume. The elderly owner had taken over after the two jackals had barged in.

Thank God they've turned in.

Gerald's pipe is smoldering in a tin tray as he runs a cloth over the reception desk. His eyebrows double-raise when I ask for a pinch of tobacco.

Evelyn can see the small exchange between us. I'm certain she'll guess it's not only about borrowing matches.

I sit more closely to my female friend this time.

How could someone manage such perfect skin throughout such a primitive upbringing? I leave it as an unspoken compliment and strike a match, bringing that familiar glimmer of blue to Evelyn's attention again.

"You have gorgeous eyes," she says. "I've never seen the color in a dark man."

I'm thankful to be occupied in the stoking of my pipe. I’m only a shade darker than she. Once it's at a steady burn, I say, "It's my father's eyes." The cherry smell of the tobacco lingers as I remember getting lost in them. "His eyes were the only way I ever really got a sense of who he was. I never knew my mother. I was brought up in a boys' home in New York. When I turned eighteen, I got into my trust and finally started living on my own." I eye the back of my hand while I keep my pipe alive. "Mostly because I was tired of having the backs of my fingers striped with a ruler."

She can tell I’m judging her reaction. Neither a nod nor a shake of the head. Just that unimpressed devilish expression of understanding. I return it, in jest.

"I visited my dad in the nursing home as often as possible, but most of what he said was more to himself than to me. His life's a puzzle. All are after Alzheimer's, I guess."

Evelyn's expression softens.

"About the time I felt that we might be getting somewhere, he was hospitalized. And when that happened, I couldn't stand it anymore. Especially with my own diagnosis. I was just getting discouraged, ya know? Looking at my future self all the time."

Now she's nodding. Her eyes pause on my clefted chin; also my father’s.

I try a draw, but the pipe has given up.

"So, I left America. Haven't gone back. That was five years ago."

We've both had heartaches.

I put down the pipe and unbutton at the collar and the cuffs.

We both have heritage.

"So, you were telling me about these quids," I say. "They could help you see the future?"

I've taken the pipe again and am lighting it. She's watching.

She laughs. "We smoked it, too." She waves her cigarette around before making a strong gesture toward the pipe, which finally had given up a little draw and was again threatening to smolder out. "Ya know, that's precisely it. How can I ever know if what occurred under the influence of the Oxychana has any natural meaning to me? On one hand, the things my mother told me rang true and still eat at me. On the other hand, I loved feeling the *real* things. The water between my toes and fingers as I searched for special little stones. Going off with Serat and climbing into the canopy, far from the village. But those things got harder the more I smoked and dreamed."

She tamps out the little cigarette.

I make no attempt to light back up. I even set my pipe aside again rather than fight with it.

"The Moon," she whispers to me and then lets her head lull before continuing. "Mother grew protective of me, and Father started sending suitors when I was fourteen; one a month, sometimes two..."

This time she's awaiting a reaction.

I offer her nothing.

"It wasn't all that," she says. "Mother turned them all away. Of course, each man had to journey through trance with her before ever getting so much as a word with me. That went on for years; Father traveling, Mother trancing."

Now, perhaps she sees a little something in my demeanor.

"What?"

I pick back up my pipe, intent on relighting it now. "It's nothing."

"Come on," she says. "What? You don't believe me?"

"No. It's… Well, I was feeling a bit guilty smoking with you, but you know, I guess this can't be as bad as chewing and toking Ganja around the clock."

She looks both relieved and ridiculed at once but presses on as I strike a match.

"A little weed is one thing—"

I look surprised at her comment.

"What? You think I haven't tried weed? Where do you think I've been living after all these years? Under a rock?"

My coal catches some fierce heat, and I cough, halfway through my overbearing draw. "I guess not!" It comes out as a croak and I do my best to stifle the coughing with some laughter.

"Heck no," Evelyn says when I've composed myself better. "Weed doesn't compare. You could wake up at any moment and remember that you had just been under the influence of Oxychana."

The way she says it makes us both go quiet and leaves me holding the pipe aloft, just staring.

"In fact, I sometimes wonder if I may wake up now!" She's visibly entertained by my worry. "Maybe my whole flight from home has been a dream?"

There's a silence, then I loosen back up a bit. "That would be some good Ganja." She smiles while I stoke the pipe. Blow a weak smoke ring. "So, how do you know it's not?"

"Good memories just need good markers," she says, eyeing her ring finger. "I wasn't running back home after Adam left me."

For the first time, I spy the pale loop on her finger, like scar tissue. Reminiscent of her heartaches. No need to ask who he was to know that we both are aware of sharing a common ailment. Loss.

Evelyn sees my eyes fixed on it, and she reaches over touching the spot.

"War," she says simply. "It takes those most precious to us, yet promises liberation."

Our attention is caught when Gerald drops his pouch of tobacco onto the coffee table in front of me in a gesture of hospitality. He nods to us both, switches off the stained glass lamp, and settles with a book behind the counter.

I oblige the offer, repacking the pipe, so Evelyn will know she has my undivided time. She had lit another cigarette, drew on it, then laid it in the ashtray.

"You wouldn't believe how much war resembles the sound of urban development. Serat and I were the only ones brave enough to go so far from home to see tractors and trucks... foresting operations. The gunfire was just another thing for us to explore.

"Jackhammers, dynamite... it wasn't Adam we expected to find. And when we came across him armed and limping, Serat didn't want me to have anything to do with him. Of course, I was more excited than anything else. His eyes were blue like yours, but he was white.

"My debate was that Mother would have everything needed to repair his leg, but Serat forbid we bring him back to the village. My English was broken at best, but Adam's French was well enough. I'll never forget the look Serat gave me before leaving me there with him—"

Evelyn mimes lifting a palm frond and peeking beneath, "—eyes peering back at me, like a jaguar from the jungle."

She goes quiet then, leaning on her right elbow, her knuckle to her lips.

I try envisioning it. "This was during the Biafrican war?" I ask.

"Later, I found out that's what it was. There were missionaries preaching to the outlying villages, just outside of the base Adam was stationed at. I didn't know that was what was going on, or even that it was what was causing the unrest. Not until later did I figure out why there was guerrilla warfare happening that close by." She looks me in the eyes. "I was a potential convert, now that I think of it. No." She drops into the memory. "It was more than that. It became much more than that."

Evelyn's cigarette had burned itself down to the filter while resting on the edge of the copper tin. I flip it into the ashtray and set my pipe down on the end table. "So did Serat—you said that was her name, bring help?"

Evelyn takes her knuckle away and opens her palm. "He. Yes. And if he did, I wasn't there."

"You left like that?"

She sits up, visibly trying to compose herself. After a moment, she seems to steady.

"Okay," I say. "I think it's that time. Let me help you upstairs."

She gives me a devilish grin.

"I could sit here with you all night. Really, I could, but the gentleman in me says we should take a raincheck."

She's bracing herself with her right hand on the sofa and puts her left hand out daintily.

I stand, pocket my pipe, and take her hand. When I'm reaching for the pouch of tobacco, a tisking sound comes from Gerald's direction. I look over, and the man is motioning for me to forget it. I do so, and hoist Evelyn to her feet, bringing her into a brief and clumsy embrace. Then steadied, I spread my arm toward the steps.

As we climb, Evelyn uses her free hand to hold up the hem of her skirt and says, "It was never Adam's intention to go back with us. I knew it. He knew it. Truthfully, I was trying to get rid of Serat. I knew what I was doing, as selfish and childish as it was."

We top the stairs, and I look at her.

"I didn't have time to think about how much I may have been hurting my mother by leaving. I was toting Adam through the jungle toward his base." She trails off then says in a blend of French and English, "The cherry blossoms, the painting, land of our own..."

She had paused and was looking into my face. I nod empathetically, then grip her biceps, going to her eye level. "Are," I say, looking directly into her eyes, "you gonna make me do the dance?"

She shakes her head and smiles. "Room ten, silly."

With her arm over my shoulder, we start down the hall toward the far window where the deep crimson of morning is already playing at the stained glass. She puts her weight against me. I hitch her up tall again. "Let's move, soldier."

She plays along, even laughs. It's nice, laughing again. When we reach the door, Evelyn reaches into the bosom of her gown and takes the opportunity to catch me following her hand with my eyes. Her shoulders do a dance. I follow them up and her face is scrunched up, the lips pursed. Then out comes the key. She holds it briefly aloft, satisfied that she has my eyes under her control now, then begins working the lock.

Just then, the neighboring door comes open, and a young girl in pin-striped shorts backs into the hall. The smell of patchouli and hibiscus emanates from the room. She's tugging on bedsheets like a puppy. There's giggling from inside and out. The young lady stops when she sees the two of us at Evelyn's door and puts a hand up to cover her mouth and nose. Another attractive and dainty woman, this one blonde and a bit taller, comes into the hall holding the other end of the sheet, which seems to be the only thing covering her unmentionables.

Evelyn and I look at one another. Then the two girls go back into the room as a single unit, shuffling their feet and closing the door. We both laugh.

"Looks like it's gonna be a lonely morning," I say.

“Try not to get depressed,” she says, then steps across her threshold and pushes the door partly closed. "I'd invite you in, but..."

"No. Of course not," I say, blushing a little. "Um, until tomorrow, well, today, I guess then, Miss."

The last thing I see is one of her green eyes in the crack before the door clicks gently closed.

Giggling is coming from room twelve again. Lying there beside my coat on top of the bedspread, I see clearly now these girls whose giggling has plagued my nights. Staring at the ceiling, I wonder if Evelyn hears it too. She surely does, being right across the hall. Now, I'm thinking of my own question. "Are you jealous?" I roll over to one side and clutch a pillow to me. I am tonight.

I see the tumbler on the table, sitting perfectly where she had left it, a smudge from her tender lips occupying the rim. More giggling, passionately this time, floats through the thin walls of the establishment. I can't help but imagine them. Grabbing up the neck of my coat, I turn quickly off the side of the bed and throw it over the back of the mahogany chair.

"Damn it!" Though I only had taken a small dose of cough medicine, it had still produced its stimulant effect, and I was tempted to take another glass of scotch. My ivory fingernails are prominent against the crystal as I lift the glass, but it's not these that I'm eyeing. God! It's the smudge! I can practically taste the pink of her lips.

It's only as I move to put the glass back onto the table in a single act of determined will that I hear the soft rapping on my door. It's much too early for staff to be doing their rounds. That's when it hits me. My pulse quickens in an instant. I pull the door open gently and dare a look, hoping my desire has been sensed through brick and mortar.

"I heard the giggling." Evelyn says. Her hair is combed straight, a light curtain of it covering her downturned face. Her feminine silhouette showing through the sheer slip of faded pink material. "I couldn't help it." She says. Then her eyes rising, "Couldn't help ask myself if I—"

Our eyes meet. "—were jealous?" I say with her. Then the heat running beneath my skin is felt between us.

"Yes," she says.

Immediately, I capture her. Pulling the door open and drawing her close to me in a flame of desire. The door closes, and I'm with her, turning her toward the bed as her hands make their way to my face. Then I feel kisses there, and on my lips. Then my neck. I tuck my stomach in when I feel her hands at my belt.

As her fingers worked, I felt a guilty side effect of the medicine—a certain detachment, a dulling of physical sensation that was the cruel trade-off for mental clarity.

Worry rose briefly and I paused to breathe into her hair as she focused on the buckle. It clinks gently and I begin to explore her slip. She looks up and takes in my expression as my hands do their work. Following the contour of her. The hardened nipple. I resist groping but can see in her face that she wants me to own it. So, I do and all fear of my impotence melts away.

We tumble onto the bed. Her slip up and my mouth having found its mark. The thin white cloth of her panties stretch in my right hand and slide down.

Her hands are busy again. One grasping at my belt while the other has untucked my shirt and slipped in wrist deep. I help her. Our motions urgent and needy.

Once we free ourselves from the tangle of half-shed clothes, I take a moment to appreciate the smooth, caramel expanse of her thighs. She watches me through hooded eyes, her chest heaving with anticipation.

I lower myself to her, our bodies fitting together like puzzle pieces. Her fingers dig into my shoulders as I press into her, and she arches up to meet me. We move together, lost in the rhythm of our desire.

Afterward, we lie in each other's arms, spent and sated. Evelyn's head on my chest, her hair a spray of fine fiber across my skin. There is a black cord around her neck. The only thing she still wears. I run my fingers along it. It's a simple crescent moon, the metal warm from her body heat.

"What's the story behind this?" I ask softly, careful not to disturb the peaceful moment.

Evelyn shifts, her hand coming up to cover mine. "It's a family heirloom," she murmurs. "Passed down from my mother, and her mother before her. They say it is the key to the wisdom of the moon."

I nod, intrigued but not wanting to push, so just watch her drift off to sleep.

I couldn't join her in slumber, not yet. The medicine wouldn't allow it—sleep, another of its casualties. Instead, I lay beside her, memorizing the pattern of her breathing, the exact curve of her shoulder in the morning light. I carefully remove my jotting pad from the nightstand and sketch it. Surely, I wouldn't forget this! Then I draw the pendant.

Finally, resigned to likely need a dose of the medicine in the morning, I sneak briefly from the bed and take a long draw from the bottle of scotch then pour a glass of water to keep at bedside. I climb back in close to her and shut my eyes, watching little clear ghosts do swirls in the dark. Until sleep finally captures me, I wonder what she dreams.

V. EVELYN DREAMS OF NIGERIA, 2022

Evelyn's heart was pounding as she trudged through the damp air, pulling Adam along with her. The rain had started, and her knees ached under her soaked kanga from stumbling so much of the way. Adam frequently pulled her down behind the fronds when gunfire pierced the air, stilling the curious sounds of the wilderness. It was like a devil's cry to Evelyn, but she held fast to him and allowed him to take in the whole sight of her.

Her face, so prominent against the moist leaves of the emerald forest, was soothing to his pain. The colorful garb, now riddled with mud, had matted to her body, making her unmistakably different, but in no way uncivilized. How becoming she was in her wet clothing. Normally loose and concealing, now it clung form-fitting to her lovely figure.

"One day, you will unite with a man born of the sun," her mother's voice boomed in her mind. She blocked it out.

Adam sat with his back to a twisted old fallen tree, now decaying and host to a family of fern growth. Sliding up the tree and cocking his head back, he looks into the undergrowth ahead of them for movement. The pop of rifle rounds had grown close. "There's two, maybe three at most," he says. Then pulls a large knife from its sheath on his belt and presses it firmly into her hand. He phrases in French, so she understands. "Just in case."

"In case?" she asks him, looking into his eyes now, showing worry for the first time.

"If they take me. They won't shoot you, not a lady, but they may get close enough, and you may have to..." her look tells him she understands. Just then, a commotion alarms them in time to make out a yellowish shape beyond some prayer plants. The leaves shuffle violently, and the moss scatters as Evelyn gasps. Adam moves to swing the rifle from around his back when a flurry of red feathers is joined by the horrible sound of a jungle cat's screams.

A jaguar pounced, had the bird, and was leaping off into the trees before Adam had completely readied his defense. Both of them lay in the leaves paralyzed by the disruption. When they heard the sound of gunfire moving off, they turned to one another and dared to breathe. Then slowly, they put their heads together and started to laugh with relief.

Their spirits had risen but the brush was still a gnarly mass and the rain was breaking through the canopy in waterfalls. Adam seemed to have regained some of his strength, and they moved quickly behind where the cover was thickest. They had covered miles, and the dark was threatening to be upon them at any moment. Palmettos hacked off at the base had been their only guide, and here they were surrounded by them. "We're close," he whispers, pointing through the night at what seemed like a void carved into the forest wall. "We should be within a half mile of the border, but there's hardly any cover beyond the breach of the forest."

She looked at him questionably, "But we have seen no one."

He glances her direction with a finger to his lips. "They're out there. The problem is, nobody knows we are coming. I'll have to alert them, stay here, and be ready."

Adam's hair complimented him consummately, and she could envision it well washed and tended to. The long golden locks, now darkened by the weather, were a rare sight in the jungle.

She watches as he moves away, barely letting his limp impede his movement. He is a man of strength in the large world, she thinks to herself, a man without fear. He had slung his rifle back over his shoulder and gone beyond the giant elephant ear leaves that acted like gutters to the downfall of water from above. He disappeared, his camouflage hiding him well from prying eyes.

She became aware of the jungle's liveliness again, as the dark enveloped and her eyes grew accustomed. Sounds of all the native birds and insect varieties took on a blanket effect in the night. She didn't like this loneliness, on the edge of a jungle she once thought of as impenetrable, here on the cusp of everything her father had filled her head with over the years, here, on the brink of change.

A piercing whistle sliced through the night air over the sounds of the rain, and Adam burst from the leaves reaching for her arm with an eagerness that made her forget his injuries. He tugged her to her feet and started toward the darkness of the open air where she now saw a light in the distance too high to be natural. "Go now!" barked Adam as gunfire paraded from the forest only yards from where they'd emerged.

It was then she saw the silver and gold lights coming from the jungle in a steady stream toward the sky. Her mind had no time to recount the New Year's fireworks her father spoke of from his travels to Asia, but it was the same. She would not let go of Adam. When he turned and aimed in the direction they'd come, she ignorantly yanked him along. The piercing wail of another firework was blurring her train of thought, but she vaguely made out structures in the dark, and before long saw the twists of wire with spiked barbs coiled around wood. "I see something!" She managed to say among the noise, not knowing if he heard, or if he cared.

Gunshots from behind rang out one after another, and the ground sprang to life around them. Leaf and mud spattering in union with each shot, some bullets leaving trails through the wet terrain like whips in action. She thought of dropping but kept running until Adam's rifle came to life with a devastating sound she had never heard so close, and she stumbled in the wet mud, forcing him down to one knee, clasping her ears. Adam let loose three consecutive shots before yanking her up and pushing her forward, urging her to continue. She could make out the shape of soldiers in the distance moving closer, and as she squinted in the torrential downfall of rain to make things clearer, an explosion rocked the earth not a hundred feet distant, sending mud pelting them as they ran.

Adam was screaming in French, "I'm here! Fire! Fire!" and the horizon was lit up with an array of gunshot, brilliant enough to illuminate the source of the constant drumming she had been hearing. There stood an awning of metal built quite poorly, but finally making a distinct welcome entrance into where they were headed. Another interruption of explosion, this time nearer the forest, had obviously come from this side. They entered between wooden uprights, crowded in by men in Adam's same garb.

Evelyn looked up at the corrugated metal and listened, separating the steady drumming on the roof from all of the confusion. Through it, she blinked away teary memories of her mother playing.

VI. TRAGEDY

It seemed ages before they were finally at rest in the infirmary. The men had helped Adam onto a small rover amidst heated arguments, whose subject matter had been obvious to Evelyn. Yet Adam had persevered and kept her by his side. Assuring her it would all be okay, and comforting her through every mishap, explaining quietly what she was seeing for the first time in her life. Though the storm was thundering all around, she was wide-eyed at the extraordinary things she beheld. The vehicle they traveled in at uneasy speeds, and the light she had seen from the darkness emanating from a tower of smooth rock, sealed tight with glass which sent the water streaming down instead of letting into the establishment.

The building they were now in was even more intriguing. The floors made of fine white tiles with partially reflective surfaces. Beds of smooth clean cotton, and soft pillows held off the ground on steel metal frames with wheels, allowing them to glide freely from place to place. Trinkets of all types occupied the shelves and drawers. A steady cream material called plastic housed a variety of medical tools, which they used as they tended to Adam as she watched. The place's smell made her uneasy at first, but she knew they were safe. Never had she seen a place so uniform, so entirely closed in, yet so massive. Everywhere she looked was clean and white and new, a completely different world from the outside where the rains had begun to calm. If she hadn't just come through the foreboding forest and into this white haven, illuminated by soft electrical lights, she may never know it was dark outside right now. Only the small square portholes that gave view to outside were the bit of evidence to the time of day.

Lovely women in pure white attended him, and one took Evelyn by the hand and led her to a small room with polished metal fixtures that she explained were to run water and bathe. A fresh change of clothes was left on the counter for her with a towel. Evelyn looked into the mirror above the sink and saw herself as she would often be found as a child, covered in filth from head to toe and her hair in disarray. "Oh, what mother would say to me now." She thought to herself as she untwisted the fabric of her kanga and began peeling the stiffened material from her body. She turned the knob in the shower and smiled as the water cascaded down in thin streams. Steam began to rise, and she put her hand first into the wonderful jet before immersing herself in it joyfully.

Evelyn had taken a whole twenty minutes in the washroom, but had managed to brush her teeth and pull the knots from her hair with her fingers. When she emerged, she saw Adam sitting upright and speaking to a very tall, dark, bearded man in pressed camouflage. The man was decorated with gold pendants and striped with colored material. He was gesturing to Adam to take the keys from his hand when Adam's eyes fell upon her.

The gown she adorned was but a simple white thing, with buttons up the chest to the collar, which she had failed to fasten. But her skin was so beautiful. Her green eyes were piercing, and the way the corners of her mouth turned naturally up upon his glance made his gaze all too noticeable to his visitor.

"Evelyn!" Adam says, taking the keys from the man. "Colonel, here she is now." He winces and braces himself on the metal framework as he takes his feet, secretly waving her to come near.

Approaching the Colonel, she realizes how tall the man really is, inches taller than Adam and a good foot above her. The man's eyes were yellowed but still wide, not weary in the least. Another great man of power, she thinks to herself.

The man reaches slowly and takes her hand gently, lifting it before him, saying, "I am indebted to you, miss. You must be quite exhausted from lugging our Adam home?" He turns his head to Adam and makes a gesture hard for her to see, then continues, "You are quite brave."

Evelyn bows her head to him, unsure of what to say, and Adam saves her. "Yes. Evelyn, this is Colonel Mohammed. He has agreed to let you stay here, with me, if it would be comfortable for you. I have quite a lodge not far from here; there is plenty of room. Of course, if you would like to go back..."

Her soul sinks for a moment at the thought, and she is adamant when she speaks, "No. I could not see leaving your side now. At least until your wounds are healed. You will not be going back into battle immediately, will you?"

With this, the Colonel laughs. “Not our bravest warrior,” he says and Adam looks away as if they shared some inside joke. Then the colonel pats her hand. "Just as I said, a strong woman. Were it her, she would be back there this coming morning." He laughs again and lets her hand fall. "I can see you have much to learn, and Adam will have plenty of time to show you around. Our home is yours as long as you'd like." Mohammed turns to Adam and puts a strong hand on his shoulder. "I'm glad you're back, my friend. Get some rest. God bless." He tips the camouflage covering on his head in gesture on his way to the door. "My lady."

"Are you not going to bathe?" Evelyn asks Adam. Though his wound had been cleaned and sutured, then wrapped in gauze, the rest of him was still covered in filth. His left pant leg had been simply torn away in order to work with his injuries.

"Not here. I would much rather be home where I have a fresh change of clothes and my very own shower." He reaches over to the bedside counter and grabs a black leather-bound book with golden pages. "My Bible." He says, folding it into his chest. "Mohammed brought it to me." He sees she doesn't quite understand and immediately has an urge to help her find comfort here. All cleaned up, he can tell she is young, perhaps seventeen. He takes the crutch beside the bed in his left arm and tucks it under his armpit, when the idea hit. With an extremely mischievous grin, he looks to her and says, "Hey, wanna drive a car?"

Adam and Evelyn were inseparable. Besides the occasional run to the annex for snacks, they were never apart. It had been more than six months since she had found him in the jungle, and since that time she'd soaked up much knowledge on the present era. The stories Adam would tell her, and the pictures he would show her, overshadowed her father's tales and eventually smoothed the memory of them from the forefront of her mind. Adam was easily thirty years old, but from the time he stepped out of the washroom after coming from the jungle, she was captivated by him. His hair so sheen, golden like the center point of a daisy, his eyes like cobalt stone.

At the start, she would wrap his leg and sit patiently by the light of the antique lamp as he read from the Bible, translating words she didn't understand to French for her. Time passed and they fell more in love with hearing one another speak. He would explain the creation of the Earth in detail to her from his scripture. How in the beginning, the earth was formless and empty, darkness was over the surface of the deep, and the Spirit of God was hovering over the waters. He went on to explain that God created masses of dry ground he called land, and eventually Man and Woman. This great debate was a steady constant in their relationship, and they both found exponential growth in one another's knowledge, for their stories always complemented one another.

Evelyn would eventually tell Adam of the Oxychana practice and the visions she had. She told him of her earliest encounter with the Earth Mother at age eight, and both she and Adam reveled in the astonishing similarities of their creators.

"It is funny that your beliefs begin above the waters. Ours begin within them. As the water itself is the deity." She would explain

She explained how these waters were imbued with consciousness of the Mother and that torrent upon torrent of indescribably fast movement within herself produced friction and heat and eventually fire. That the fire could not mix with the surrounding waters and fought its way to the surface, exploding forth and bringing with it steam which became the air, and the cooling fires on the surface became the earth. She explained that this was only possible through the Earth Mother's will and that man carried with him this same will, which her people called 'the fire to live'. He was astounded when she went on to explain that her people believe that each human being is but a perfect reproduction of the Earth Mother, and that their bodies are alive in the same way that she is.

He would counter with a scripture from his Bible: Then God said, 'Let us make mankind in our image, in our likeness, so that they may rule over the fish in the sea and the birds in the sky, over the livestock and all the wild animals, and over all the creatures that move along the ground'. And they would laugh together and connect on an unseen level.

They had long conversations about other countries and their beliefs, and he found it particularly interesting that her tribe saw the separation of Pangea into the landforms today a result of man's modern ways of segregation, especially racially. It was then that he sparked a deep untold interest in her and began thinking passionately about her. He learned her on Alfred Wegener and his discovery of plate tectonics and compared their theories on the movement of landmasses. They were one another's teacher, and before long, she had begun speaking English quite well.

It was on the night that Adam had slipped climbing from the shower with his knee that was still too weak, that she fell for him entirely. She found him naked on the bathroom floor with but a towel pulled loosely over him to hide his more private parts. She had already gotten into one of the many lavish nightgowns he had purchased for her that they had picked out together. She knelt beside him in the puddled water, unconcerned for her gown, shaking him softly. He was looking up at her. Water had traveled up the light blue material of her gown, and he found himself moving in a way that she could see him exposed. Her eyes sought the towel and the exposed flesh of his inner thigh, and when they turned back to his face, her cheeks in a blush, his lips were waiting.

The cherry blossoms were in full bloom, and the sun was shining warmly overhead on the day of their wedding. The white chairs and lattice gazebo on the green lawn, and the pink trees among them, were a sight to behold. Mohammed gave her away, and they were united in holy matrimony under God, who she'd come to know well through Adam.

Evelyn's heart was filled with both joy and trepidation. She'd looked into Adam's eyes, those cobalt pools that had captured her heart, and whispered, "Promise you will never leave me."

Adam's gaze had softened, and he'd squeezed her hands gently. "I cannot promise that, my love. But I promise I will always come back to you."

Evelyn had felt a lump form in her throat, but she'd nodded, understanding the weight of his words. They'd sealed their vows with a kiss, and as the cherry blossoms floated around them, she had prayed that their love would be enough to keep him safe.

In the following days, Adam began walking without so much as a limp, and by the end of 2022, when the war was in a state of stalemate, they received word that Mohammed was granted increased British support. The

Nigerian federal forces were to launch their final offensive against the Biafrans on December twenty-third. It was to be a major thrust by the 3rd Marine Commando Division and commanded by Colonel Obasanjo. Obasanjo was to become president if the attack succeeded in splitting the Biafran enclave into two by the end of the year. Mohammed was very close with Obasanjo and found this to be an opportunity for more power. However, he did not want Obasanjo to be a cruel leader, so he had already begun swaying him on the side of Christianity. Adam was asked to serve alongside Mohammed one last time. He would never return.

The nights were lonely for Evelyn, and the days were long. She would pass her time reading Adam's books and twisting the wedding ring on her finger as if wishing on it to bring him home. There had been no word from the south for almost a month, and she was growing weary with worry. Being alone left her to think of her mother and father, who now seemed light-years away, though she could cover the distance by truck in less than an hour, if such trails existed. She started a hobby of painting. She had gone to the annex to pick up more canvas the day she heard that the war had ended. It was January 15, 2023.

Evelyn stood in front of her canvas and easel, making small strokes with a fine brush, trying to bring out the highlights in his eyes. She wanted it perfect for him when he returned. Mohammed watched her from the window by the entrance, leaning her face close to the canvas, completely enthralled. He didn't want to knock, but he knew it would eventually have to be done. Evelyn sensed something and grew still. It had been but a few days since word of the war's end, and she was expectantly waiting on her husband's return. Then she heard the knock on the door, "Just like Adam!" she thought to herself. Her heart skipped a beat, and she smiled cheek to cheek then she dashed to the door.

She held the hem of her dress and her paintbrush with her left hand and the wooden palette in her right. Moving the brush to her right hand and gripping it with her thumb, she flipped the latch and slung the door open with bright eyes. Mohammed stood in the doorway with his hands outstretched to her, and the blood ran from her cheeks as she realized what he held. The wooden palette slipped from her hand and clattered on the stone floor. There, in his hands, was Adam's Bible.

VII. FIRST ENCOUNTER

I awoke under the shadows of trees, my head throbbing and mind foggy. No, not trees—the canopy of the four-poster bed at the Brunswick Inn. For a disorienting moment, I couldn't remember how I'd gotten here, or why there was a warm weight pressed against my side. Then the fog parted enough. Evelyn's dark hair spread across my chest, her arm draped possessively over my waist.

Last night. The intensity of the connection. The struggle against the medicine's dampening effects. The sweet release when I'd finally, gloriously, overcome the chemical barrier. I dared a smile. Then I saw the jot pad on the nightstand by an empty glass. On it was the picture of a moon pendant. No artistic talent in that drawing by any means; simply a memory, hurriedly scratched.

I drew open the drawer and the thunk of the cough medicine bottle against the inside made Evelyn stir. I winced at the coming evening, considered my exhaustion, but resisted, putting the pad into the drawer and closing it gently.

I glance back at Evelyn's closed eyelids. The high light of near noon was filtering through the curtains, casting a soft glow across the room. She's pulled her knees up close to her body as if seeking comfort in her dreams. Carefully, I slide out of bed, trying not to disturb her. Pull the comforter tight around her and place a gentle kiss on her temple before throwing on my robe and making my way down to the lobby.

To my surprise, the thermos of tea that's usually set out in the mornings is still there. It's probably settled, but it'll do. I pour myself a cup and drain it. Still warm. Then pour two proper ones, stirring in a bit of milk, and take a moment to enjoy the peaceful atmosphere. Everyone else must already be about their daily grinds. It seemed as if we were the only ones who'd slept through the morning.

Returning, topping the steps, two cups of tea in hand, I encounter the girls from room twelve. The one in the lead, dressed in denim jeans, a fur-collared coat, and black gloves, gives me a smile as they approach. I step back against the wall, holding the cups close to my body as they pass by in a tight-knit group. The other girls eye the tea and exchange giggles, no doubt remembering our own orchestra of sounds competing with theirs last night.

Once they're gone, I can't help but smirk at the cups in my hands. Juggling them carefully, I open the door and step inside. Evelyn is still asleep, her dark hair splayed across the pillow like a halo. I set one cup on the bedside table and ease myself into a chair, content to watch her for a moment. I take a sip. Yes, warm but all hopes of visible steam are gone. I spend a little time on my cell phone and let her continue dozing a while. Can't get any worse, I think, taking another sip.

Then, unable to resist any longer, I reach out and gently shake her shoulder. "Evelyn, wake up, sleepyhead."

She stirs, turning with a smile. "Morning," she says, her voice husky with sleep.

"Hardly. Noon, more like. I brought you some tea," I say, holding out the cup. "It might be a little thin, but it's better than nothing."

She sits up, clutching the comforter to her chest, and takes the cup from my hands. "Full service," she says. Then that devilish look from last night.

I lean back in my chair, cradling my own cup. "Taste it before looking so impressed," I say.

We sat in silence for a moment, sipping our tea and watching the dust motes dance in the sunbeams. But as the seconds tick by, I can see a shadow passing over Evelyn's face.

"What's wrong?" I ask, setting my cup aside, but I already had guessed. "Bad dreams?"

She hesitates, then shakes her head. "Not bad, exactly. Just... memories." She looks out the window, her gaze distant. "I was back in the infirmary with Adam, when he introduced me to Mohammed."

I nod, remembering the story. The loss of her husband, the uncertainty of her future. It was a lot to take in last night.

"You don't have to talk about it if you don't want to," I say gently. "But I'm here if you need me."

She gives me a grateful smile and reaches out to squeeze my hand. "I know. And I appreciate it. It's just... hard, sometimes. Remembering everything I've lost."

We lapse into silence again, but it's not uncomfortable. There's an understanding between us now, a shared sense of grief and longing.

Eventually, Evelyn sets her empty cup aside and stretches, the comforter slipping down to reveal the smooth expanse of her back. "I should probably get dressed," she says, glancing over her shoulder at me. "What's on the agenda for today?"

I grin, feeling a sudden thrill of excitement. "Well," I say, standing up and moving to the closet. "I was thinking we could catch a show tonight. There's this great little theater out in Windsor, the Theatre Royal. According to Tesla's Nightout App, it's five stars, and the transportation is included. I Google Earthed it. It's not much to look at from the outside, but the reviews are all positive."

Evelyn's eyes light up at the idea. "That sounds fun," she says, swinging her legs over the side of the bed. "I haven't been to a theater in ages. Everything is so digital nowadays. The spheres are cool, but you can't beat authentic theater. What app is that?"

"Nightout," I show her the screen of my phone. "You just put in the time and check off your interest and it lines up the attractions, meals, and transportation. See."

She looks at the map and sees the little Tesla logos moving around on it. "Like Uber?"

"Yeah, but all inclusive. Better, it accommodates our vices. Well, except in the car, of course."

"Interesting," she says and gives that pert little smile. "It's a date then."

When I arrived in the lobby, I'd been slightly rejuvenated by a cold shower and that second cup of tea, all the way down to the dregs. Evelyn comes down the steps, wearing a deep red coat that hugs her curves, with thigh-high boots and black leggings that showcase her long, lean legs. A wide-brimmed black hat sits atop her dark cascade of silken locks, giving her an air of mystery and sophistication.

"You look incredible," I say, offering her my arm. "Shall we?"

She slips her hand into the crook of my elbow with a smile. "Lead the way."

The ride to Windsor is a blur of snowy fields and frosted windows. We sit close together in the back seat. Evelyn's head was resting on my shoulder, and I hid a yawn as she watched the countryside roll by. A valet rode in the passenger seat as the vehicle navigated the roads via satellite.

When we arrive at the theater, the valet opens our doors for us and I can see Evelyn's eyes widen in surprise. Despite its unassuming exterior, the inside is a marvel of plush red velvet and gleaming oak. The seats are arranged in a sweeping arc, rising up from the stage like the petals of a flower.

"It's beautiful," Evelyn breathes, her hand tightening on my arm. "I can't believe I've never been here before."

We make our way down to our seats, just a few rows back from the stage. As we settle in, I catch a glimpse of familiar faces a few rows behind us. A light laughter lifts from the trio.

"Don't look now," I murmur, leaning in close to Evelyn's ear, "but I think we've been spotted by our new friends from room twelve."

She glances over her shoulder, her eyes widening as she takes in the sight of the man in the purple suit, surrounded by the three giggling girls from the Brunswick. "Oh my," she says, turning back to me with a grin. "Looks like we're not the only ones with a taste for the finer things."

“I'll try and pretend I'm not jealous,” I say. I take her hand in mine, giving it a gentle squeeze. "Maybe we should invite them to join us for a drink after the show," I suggest, only half-joking.

Evelyn laughs and shakes her head. "Maybe I want you all to myself tonight."

I grin and bring her hand to my lips, pressing a kiss to her knuckles. "Whatever you wish, my lady."

As the lights dim and the curtain rises, I glance back over my shoulder and see the strange man’s eyes have settled on me. I reach into my pocket and thumb the lid of the medicine bottle. I have a feeling this is not going to be an early night and begin watching for an opportunity to covertly take a substantial dose.

I feel better just knowing I will soon be more alert. For now, I'm exactly where I'm meant to be. If I can only hold on to these memories…

The play ends, and the lights come on. The story of love, both within and outside the bonds of marriage, has struck a chord with me. I've been stealing glances at Evelyn, her face flushed with emotion, and I know she's felt it too.

We linger in our seats as the rest of the audience files out, content to bask in the afterglow of the performance. But eventually, when the custodians come in, we rise. Hand in hand, sidling from our row and pacing our way up the aisle toward the lobby, where the cast is already mingling with their adoring fans.

As we stepped into the crowded space, I caught sight of him. It's the man from before, the one in the purple suit, surrounded by his entourage of giggling girls. They're deep in conversation, their heads bent close together, but as we approach, they look up and spot us.

"Darling!" the man calls out, his face splitting into a grin.

I look at Evelyn, sure she must know him, then realize he is addressing me.

"And his lovely consort."

I feel Evelyn's hand tighten in mine, and I give her a reassuring squeeze. "Sorry?" I say, extending my free hand. "Do we know each other?"

He takes my hand and shakes it firmly, his grip cool and dry. "I thought with the way you were looking at my girlfriends..." he says, his golden eyes sparkling. The girls titter and nod, their eyes roving over us with a kind of hunger that makes me feel like a prime cut of meat. I clear my throat and shift uncomfortably, but Evelyn seems unfazed.

"Uh," I eye the girls. "We ran into each other in the hall at the hotel," I finally offer.

His smile returns and his cane taps me lightly on the thigh. He let's go of my hand and says, "Indeed. I'm playing coy. You should be the ones insulted. They've not stopped talking about you since I picked them up at the Brunswick."

I breathed more easily.

"Girls, don't make me a weirdo," he says, half grabbing my hand again and giving it a limp little shake. "I'm Greg," he says, then gestures to the girls, who are watching us with undisguised curiosity. "Oh, c'mon, don't pretend you've not met."

"Of course," the blonde one says, her voice warm and friendly. "Sorry, you're just such a charming couple. I'm Emily." She points. "Veronica and Jessica."

Evelyn began introducing herself to the girls and Greg laughed, clapping his hands in delight.

"I'm Jesse," I said trying not to show indifference to his flamboyance.

Greg's expression went stoic, then he leaned close and said in a false whisper, "Well, I have a thing for showmanship myself. When you've got your hands in as many entertainment cookie jars as I do, you develop an eye for quality productions." I half expected another 'darling'. He adjusted his cravat with obvious satisfaction.

Evelyn eyed me when the trio went into their signature giggling. We shared a secret smile.

"Oh, he keeps us very entertained," Veronica said with a theatrical flourish.

"Always has something spectacular up his sleeve," Emily added, while Jessica nodded enthusiastically.

"Speaking of which," Veronica continued, "Next big event? Greece!"

Greg's eyes lit up with unmistakable pride. "Ah, yes. The most spectacular circus you'll ever lay eyes on." He gestured with the brass tip of his cane toward a pillar where a flyer was posted. "I happen to be invested in the venue—an ancient coliseum, actually. Been preparing it for months."

Evelyn's eyes widened, and I could feel the excitement thrumming through her. Or maybe it was my own hot-blooded memories mixing with the potion. One of those few special ones that stuck around since childhood. The tingling rose to my head.

"A real circus?" I said, honestly intrigued. "I find it a shame that the Ringling went under in the twenties. Ever since Du Soleil came on the scene, you hardly get a proper big tent experience anymore."

Greg nodded vigorously, his grin widening. "Couldn't agree more! That's precisely why this one is so special. Acrobats, fire-eaters, exotic animals—the whole magnificent spectacle. None of this modernized nonsense." He winked boldly in Evelyn's direction. "When you're vested in the venue, you can ensure authenticity."

"He's been working on this for ages," Jessica said exhaustingly. Her hand did a little Greg imitation. "Flying back and forth, coordinating everything."

"The permits alone took months," Emily added with the same light mocking.

I could see where this was going and frowned slightly, my mind racing. Greece was a long way from London, and the idea of mixing up with these relative strangers was daunting. But as I looked at Evelyn, her face alight with wonder and possibility, I felt my reservations start to crumble. Another adventure. Maybe dragons could wait.

"It sounds... intriguing," I said slowly, weighing my words.

"More than intriguing—it's going to be legendary," Greg said, leaning forward conspiratorially. "The kind of experience that changes people. Though I suppose..." He glanced at his pocket watch. "Don't think too long—the circus waits for no man."

"When exactly are we talking?" Evelyn asked, unable to hide her excitement.

"December, darling. Just in time for the winter season. The Mediterranean has its own magic that time of year."

Greg reached into his jacket and produced a small, embossed card. "Here's my number," he said, pressing it into my hand. "If you find yourselves in search of... gems."

He stood then, the girls following suit like a well-rehearsed ballet. "I do hope you'll consider it. The girls and I would be delighted to have you join us." He paused at the threshold. "After all, some opportunities only come once in a lifetime."

And then he was sweeping out of the lobby with his entourage in tow. Evelyn and I were left standing there, the card between my finger and thumb.

"What do you think?" Evelyn asked, watching them go.

I take a deep breath, trying to sort through the jumble of thoughts and emotions swirling inside me. "I think," I say, dreading having to eat when the medicine kicks in good, but tuck the card into my pocket. "That I'm hungry. Are you?"

A driverless Tesla picks us up curbside and deposits us at a little restaurant not far from the theater, a cozy spot with dim lighting and intimate booths. Greg and his companions are already there, tucked away in a corner, a bottle of wine sweating on the table between them.

We don't make our own table because Greg stands and greets us with a warm smile. "Jesse, Evelyn," he says, gesturing to the empty space in the booth beside him. "Please, join us."

I raise my hand to protest but he asks, "Nightout?"

I nod, making sense of it.

"You see?" he says waving us into the booth across from the girls, who are scattered around the table in single chairs. "We have similar tastes."

We slide into the booth, Evelyn's thigh pressing against mine in the close quarters. A waiter appears, and before I know it, there's a glass in front of us both.

The conversation flows easily, lubricated by the alcohol and the heady atmosphere. Greg regales us with tales of his travels, his voice rising and falling with the cadence of a born storyteller. The girls chime in occasionally, their laughter bright and infectious.

As the night wears on, I find myself drawn into their world. A world of wealth and privilege, of endless possibility and adventure. It's seductive, in a way, and I can feel myself getting lost in it. The drinks, the caviar, the carefree of it all. I can't help but wonder how everyone stays so alert. I survey each face. Maybe they have hidden vices of their own?

"Hazeus, Jesse," Greg says, and I pointedly think of how Evelyn pronounced it last night. "What is that devilish look for?"

I relax my eyebrows but he's already on to me. "I get it from the best," I say, diverting to Evelyn who squeezes my thigh.

"You look like a man in deep contemplation."

I take my cup considering the repercussions of more drink atop the medicine. Don't screw this up. Just remember. Whatever you do. Remember.

"Well, he's hardly finished his second glass," Evelyn says. "It's really not fair."

My wit, I think. I see something in her look. A flicker of uncertainty, of hesitation. Like she's not quite sure if I'm being honest.

I reach under the table and take her hand, lacing my fingers through hers. She squeezes back, and I lift the glass in an obvious show of obedience.

"Well, don't let me encourage you," she says.

I drink.

As the plates are cleared away and the candles burn low I start feeling better, more alive. Greg leans back in his seat and fixes us with a steady gaze. "So," he says, his voice low and intimate. "Have you given any thought to my proposal?"

Evelyn and I exchange a glance, a silent conversation passing between us. “I wasn’t aware that it was such a serious matter,” I said.

“It’s divinity, Darling,” says Greg.

“It’s friendship,” says Veronica. Emily and Jessica follow with ‘fate’ and ‘destiny’.

Then I see Evelyn, her face nodding softly in the candlelight.

"Well," I say, feeling a trill of needles at the base of my skull. "I’ve got nothing holding me down."

Greg's face spreads into a grin, and he raises his glass in a toast. "To new adventures," he says, his eyes glinting with something I can't quite name. "And to the bonds that bring us together."

“—Rather than hold us down,” says Evelyn.

We all drink. I more slowly. And as I look around the table, at these people who have so quickly become a part of our lives, I feel a sense of possibility taking root in my chest.

Maybe this is what I've been searching for all along. Not just a distraction from the pain of my past, but a chance to build something new. Something worth remembering, with Evelyn by my side. I eye the wine glass and simply wonder if I will be able to keep up.

Evelyn and I bid farewell to our extravagant host after nearly an hour of lingering in Greg's limousine parked outside the lodge. As we say our goodbyes and step into the cool London night, I take a deep breath of the crisp, autumn air. The future is uncertain, but for the first time in a long time, I'm not afraid to face it head-on.

The giggling trio were retiring to their room for the rest of the early morning, soon to be whisked away to the Mediterranean while Evelyn and I would await the date with eagerness. An enjoyable interlude, but a length of time that would slowly grow stale.

HAPPY BIRTHDAY

VIII. MOVING ON

It had been three weeks since that eventful night at the theater with Greg and the girls.

In the tranquil nights that followed, Evelyn and I savored our newfound solitude together at the Brunswick Inn. Late-night card games in my room and leisurely horse-drawn carriage rides became our favored pastimes—simple pleasures in which I found profound contentment. I had been trying to cut back on the cherry-colored cough medicine, that sweet, stringent liquid that had become as necessary to me as air. The bottle of DXM promised eight hours of clarity—eight precious hours where the fog lifted, where names stayed put in my memory, where I could be the man Evelyn deserved.

But the cycle was merciless. After those eight hours came the comedown—four hours of jittery restlessness that only scotch could smooth out. Then came morning, and with it the inevitable choice: another dose to clear the fog, or facing the day with a mind that felt like it was wrapped in cotton wool, where thoughts slipped away like minnows darting over the rim of a net.

For Evelyn, I had been trying to choose the latter more often. An undercurrent of felicity buoyed our spirits despite my private struggle—we were happy, unequivocally happy. Or at least, I wanted desperately to believe we were.

With each passing day, I grew more attuned to the nuances of her demeanor, as she, in turn, became keenly perceptive of the subtle clues hinting at my faltering memory.

"You asked me that already, Jesse," she said one morning over breakfast, her tone gentle but her eyes betraying a flicker of concern. "Just ten minutes ago."

I stared at my half-eaten toast, embarrassment flooding my cheeks. "Did I? I'm sorry."

It was day three without the medicine. My temples throbbed with a dull, persistent ache, and the world had taken on a slightly blurred quality, as if I were viewing everything through a pane of frosted glass. I'd been up since five, unable to sleep through the fog of withdrawal, downing three cups of bitter coffee in a futile attempt to sharpen my mind.

Evelyn reached across the table, her fingers intertwining with mine. "It's alright. You asked if I wanted to visit the National Gallery today."

"And what did you say?" I attempted a smile, trying to mask my growing unease, fighting the urge to excuse myself and give in. Just a small sip—enough to burn through this mental haze, to give me back the clarity I needed to be fully present with her.

"I said I'd love to, but after we visit that little bookshop you mentioned yesterday. The one with the first editions of Twain." Her smile was warm, forgiving, but I caught the shadow that passed across her face—concern mingled with something deeper, something that looked unsettlingly like fear.

I nodded, grateful for her patience, for the way she gently steered our conversations back on track when my mind wandered down forgotten paths. There were many times I failed to summon the names of the three lively young women who had resided just down the hall—Emily, Jessica, and Veronica. Their identities, so simple and similar, had proven maddeningly elusive for me.

And yet, Evelyn's essence remained indelibly etched upon the canvas of my mind. Her mother's name—Mohami, the moon—was also fixed in my recollection; notes taken among the growing collection of scribbles on the small pad I kept in the nightstand. I had once asked Evelyn about her tribe's relentless, lifelong search for the man of the sun, and she had smiled wistfully, saying, "The moon is only a reflection of the sun's light, you know?" I'd countered that Mohami must have shined with the same self-radiance as her daughter.

"Perhaps," she said. Then she told me the poem. It also went into my notes.

"The sun is filled with shining light that blazes far and wide. The moon reflects the sunlight back but has no light inside. Would you not rather be the sun that shines so bold and bright, than be the moon that only glows with someone else's light?"

I heard something in the prose. In the way she delivered it and then grew thoughtful. I was overly self-involved, too wrapped up in my own struggles to fully perceive what she might be trying to tell me. Those eyes, surveying me, as if they were expecting an answer to her riddle.

I could give none. Could only assure her that some things I would never forget. No matter how bad my memory got, never her. But slices of reality are harsh.

At night, I often awoke in a cold sweat, panic clawing at my throat as I struggled to remember where I was, who was sleeping beside me. I'd reach for my notepad in those moments, the words I'd written becoming lifelines in the darkness. Sometimes Evelyn would stir, her eyes finding mine in the dim light from the window.

"It's alright," she'd whisper, her hand cool against my cheek. "I'm here. You're here. We're at the Brunswick Inn in London."

And slowly, the world would right itself again, the pieces of my fragmented reality sliding back into place. In those nocturnal moments of clarity, I would be torn—reach for the bottle in my bedside drawer for the guaranteed relief it would bring, or endure the disorientation, the frightening blankness, to preserve some semblance of independence from the chemical crutch?

I had been strong in my abstinence. But, slowly, especially in mornings after a night of drinking with Evelyn, I would choose the medicine, telling myself it was just to avoid the slog of a hangover, just this once. But the cycle would begin again—eight hours of blessed clarity, followed by the jittery comedown that scotch would smooth away, followed by morning and the fog that only another dose could clear.

How long would Evelyn be patient? How many times could she reassure me before the weight of my condition—my dependency—became too much to bear?

Her frustration got the better of her as I poured from the bottle of scotch. I had barely procured it, and only in a rush before the shops closed. It was mere days before Halloween. She had wanted to surprise me with a gift, but the opportunity had slipped away when the banks closed for the evening. To her, it seemed as if I'd forgotten. It had been nearly five days since I was on the medicine again—my longest stretch yet—and my memory hadn't failed me; it had been the need for the scotch to avoid the terrible comedown which had done me in. My liquor store emergency had exposed the limits of her patience—my failing memory, my drinking, it had all become the boundary line she struggled to accept, though she tried to be understanding about my condition.

"You promised, Jesse," Evelyn said, her voice tight with restraint as she watched me pour the amber liquid into a crystal tumbler. "We talked about this yesterday, and the day before. Our Halloween celebration? Our half-birthdays?"

I stared at her blankly, the bottle suspended in mid-air. My mind scrambled for any recollection of this conversation, but all memory was covered by an echoing space where worry of withdrawal held sway "Our what?"

I finished the pour and dropped in a cube of ice, then swallowed it down. She sighed.

I crunched on the dissolving cube. The feel of having drank finally easing some of the anxiety. Then I remembered.

Halloween was going to be an unusual celebration. Evelyn didn't know her exact date of birth—only that it had occurred between spring and summer, something her mother often chided her for. "The only Moon maiden of tribal past ever to be born under a sun sign," she would say. My birthday, by contrast, was on May the 1st—Beltane, according to her tribal seasonal calendar. Our birthdays lay directly opposite Halloween on her ancestral wheel, so we had decided—since our birthdays were close together, and Evelyn had so many uncelebrated ones to make up for—that we should henceforth celebrate our half-birthdays and birthdays together, beginning with the coming Halloween.

But I had seemingly forgotten to stop. Forgotten the celebration we'd planned. It was true, but the forgetfulness was bolstered by the rotating fears of withdrawal, not by my condition. So yes, I'd forgotten everything except the desperate need for something—anything—to quiet the voice in my head screaming for the medicine that would clear the fog.

I lifted the bottle again to pour another, secretly thankful my cough medicine was delivered by DHL. I always forwarded my address for that matter alone.

Evelyn reached for her small purse on the nightstand, pulling out a folded slip of paper. "The reservation. At Claridge's. I'd been looking forward to it." Her voice caught, and she crumpled the paper in her fist. "I reminded you this morning when we were planning our day."

"Evelyn, I—" Guilt surged through me, sharp and bitter. I set down the bottle, moving toward her, but she stepped back, her eyes glistening. The cruel irony wasn't lost on me—I'd been trying to give up the medicine to be better for her, more present, more authentic. Instead, I was worse, and now this weak stent I was on. My memory was a decaying leaf, crumbling at the edges. I didn't know if any path could stop it.

"Don't." She held up a hand, and I saw it trembling slightly. "I understand what you're going through, Jesse. I do. But this..." She gestured to the bottle, to the room around us, to the space between us that suddenly seemed vast and unbridgeable. "I need to know if this is what our life will be. Me reminding you of the things that matter to us, while you..." She trailed off, shaking her head.

"While I what?" A rhetorical question. While I chose to combat my condition with chemicals that offered temporary reprieve but ultimately made things worse. While I tried and failed to be the man she needed.

"While you choose to escape rather than fight." She reached for her jacket, slung over the chair by the window. "I need some air."

"Evelyn, please—"

"I just need to think."

The door closed behind her with a soft click, leaving me alone with the bottle, the guilt, and the terrifying blankness in my mind where our plans should have been. I slumped onto the bed, my head in my hands. How many other promises had I forgotten? How many moments of joy had been erased from my memory, leaving only confusion and disappointment in their wake?

The scotch called to me, promising temporary oblivion. But what I really craved was in the bathroom cabinet—the sweet cherry syrup that would cut through this fog like a knife, give me back the clarity I needed to fix this mess I'd made. Just a sip. Just enough to remember what I'd forgotten, to be the Jesse that Evelyn had fallen in love with.

I walked to the bathroom, my steps heavy with defeat. The bottle was there, hidden behind the shaving cream, three-quarters full. I unscrewed the cap, the familiar medicinal smell rising to meet me. Eight hours of clarity. Eight hours to make things right with Evelyn, to be the man she deserved.

But as I raised the bottle to my lips, I caught my reflection in the mirror—haggard, eyes bloodshot, a shadow of the man I once was. Was this really the solution? Trading one prison for another? And what would Evelyn think if she knew that the Jesse she loved—the quick-witted, sharp-minded man who quoted poetry and made her laugh—was nothing but a chemical illusion?

With a curse, I recapped the bottle. The fear that had been my constant companion since the diagnosis surged to the surface, a tidal wave of dread that threatened to drown me. Soon, I would lose more than just small moments and casual acquaintances. I would lose Evelyn—first in my mind, and then in reality, as she realized that the man she loved was slowly vanishing, replaced by a hollow shell of forgetfulness and confusion.

I couldn't bear it. With shaking hands, I grabbed my coat and headed for the door. The bar down the street would be quiet this time of night, a place where I could lose myself for a little while, where no one would look at me with hurt and disappointment in their eyes.

The sights, smells, and sounds of the local tavern surrounded me, providing a comforting retreat into familiarity. I thumbed through the tattered copy of Merlyn by T.H. White, wondering. As tendrils of smoke from lit cigars and pipes coiled through the air, I found myself reminiscing about the many nights spent in Evelyn's company, gradually becoming acclimated to the perpetuity.

My thoughts turned, unbidden, to her alone in her room. What was she doing? Regret lanced through me as I recalled her hasty exit after snatching up her jacket. Undoubtedly, she heard my door slam shortly after. It was stupid really. Now I stared at the little bottle of cough syrup with a pang of self-recrimination. Is this what I had sought refuge for? Had I been bored?

Yet, I could not bring myself to wallow in remorse. The truth remained, maybe a moment's separation would be good for our relationship... But as usual, I had overlooked the repercussions of staunching my awareness of the present for the compulsions of my past.

Something was burrowing itself like a splinter. It grew more insistent with each passing minute. I had stormed out of the Brunswick and had crossed paths with that idiot who had been impossible to forget. He was the big one, who had come in and stared down Evelyn the first night of our meeting. When I'd seen him speaking with Gerlad, I thought he'd been on his way out to the bar as well. But looking around, he was no where to be seen.

Images from the previous weeks resurfaced, projected vividly against the dreary backdrop of the tavern... Would Evelyn had gone to the lobby to await my return, and that hungry lout still be there, hell-bent on disturbing the peace? It would be justice. But what of justice? A moment's weakness? Is a man not allowed one? I couldn't be sure.

A tremor cascaded down my spine as I recalled the unsettling encounter the first night, the gripping dread before Evelyn had acted. Tossing a rumpled bill onto the bar, I shrugged into my long coat and made my way towards the exit with precipitous steps.

The bridge rails seemed to narrow on me as I envisioned Evelyn succumbing to despair, seeking solace in more wine. Though my absence had been scarcely an hour, the mere thought of her vulnerable in such a state lashed me into a frenzy.

I hastened my stride, the thick wool of my coat whipping against my legs as I fought to suppress the impulse to break into a full sprint. Only my finely-tailored attire kept my feet at a gentlemanly pace. Had I been clad in the comfortable familiarity of my Clyde & Foster sweat suit and Pumas, I could have surrendered fully to the urgency pumping through my veins without a care.

The Brunswick Inn materialized through the veil of swirling snow. I properly guessed the unbolted door and shed my loafers at the threshold; propriety be damned. The rhythmic sluicing of Gerald's mop and the furrowed brow adorning the old man's countenance spoke volumes. My worries had been validated.

I heard Evelyn's nervous voice halfway up the flight of stairs. I cleared the fourth step from the top and saw the towering drunkard at Evelyn's door.

She was not entertaining the man. Rather she was pressing the door again and again, but he had his boot in the jamb and reached through, seizing her upper arm.

I was there in an instant.

The brief sight of her satin gown, torn at the neck was all it took before my fist hammered the man's arm and then yanked the man's collar.

I heard a gasp from the stairs. Gerald had followed me up. I saw this in a blur as the guy kicked off the wall and sent us careening across the hall. We hit with a thud. But before I had reoriented myself, he dropped to the floor in a half sitting position, slumping against the wall. There was no effort to regain his feet.

He was not able to defend himself in such a state. Still, with a handful of his greasy hair I was finding it hard not to pummel the brute.

While my opponent ebbed, my mind had grown clear with endorphins. But Evelyn—what would she think?

"Jesse!" Evelyn screamed.

And in the next second she was holding my elbow.

"Nothing happened Jesse! He only just now knocked on my door. Look at the state he's in!" She held his elbow tight, aware now of the couple down the hall, who had cracked their door to spy what was going on.

Gerald dared a few steps closer and gave a dismissive wave in the onlookers' direction.

I relaxed.

"Brett, you damn fool! I told you not to be meddling with her. You're drunk and they don't want a part of you! I should let him beat you silly." Gerald said, as the guy went through great pains to push himself upright.

Gerald gave him a stern push toward the lobby then apologized to me. "I told him, when he began blathering about her, to leave her be. He said he was going to his room. But when you came in and saw me mopping, that look in your eyes told me there was going to be trouble if he hadn't taken my advice. Ole Brett's been staying here long as I've been owner, but he has gotten worse on the drink this year. If you'd like, I could see it a proper excuse to be rid of him."

Evelyn gripped my coat and I looked at her, my anger already cooling, replaced by a wave of shame. I'd left her alone, vulnerable, all because I couldn't face my own failures. The bottle of medicine still sat in my pocket, untouched. I hadn't succumbed. The crisis itself had given me clarity. One I wished God would show me no chemical could match.

"It's fine Gerald. I think I speak for both of us when I say that it's about time we catch the train."

The old innkeeper nodded, understanding passing between us. He knew—perhaps had known from the start—that ours was a temporary refuge, a waystation on a longer journey.

As Gerald caught up with the stumbling Brett and led him away, Evelyn's grip on my coat loosened. She stood there, her gown torn, her eyes reflecting a complex mixture of emotions—relief, lingering fear, and something deeper, more resolute.

"Jesse," she said softly, her voice steadier now. "We need to talk."

I nodded, following her into her room. It was neat, orderly—a stark contrast to the chaos of my own thoughts. She sat on the edge of the bed, smoothing her gown with trembling fingers.

"I almost came to find you," she said, not meeting my eyes. "I didn't want to leave things as they were between us."

"Evelyn, I'm—"

"Please," she interrupted, finally looking up. "Let me finish. I know what you're going through is... unimaginable. And I know you're scared. God, Jesse, I'm scared too." She took a deep breath, steadying herself. "But running away isn't the answer. Not for either of us."

I sank down beside her, the mattress dipping under our combined weight. "I didn't want you to see me like this," I admitted, the words scraping my throat. "Forgetting things that matter. Forgetting moments that should be precious to us. I was ashamed."

"Do you think I expect perfection?" she asked, her voice soft but intent. "Do you think I don't understand what it means to love someone with all their flaws and fears? When I told you about my past, about Adam, about all the things I've lost... did you think less of me?"

"Of course not," I said immediately. "Never."

"Then why do you think I would think less of you?" Her hand found mine, warm and solid. "Jesse, I know what's coming. I know this disease will take pieces of you, of us. But I'm here, choosing to stay, to fight it with you."

I felt tears threaten, blinking hard to hold them back. "And what happens when I don't recognize you? When I look at you with empty eyes and ask who you are? How can I ask you to endure that?"

"You don't ask," she said simply. "I choose. Just as you would choose if our positions were reversed. Besides, someone's told me that won't happen." She leaned forward, her forehead touching mine. "But we can't do this if you keep running every time you're afraid. I need you present, even in your fear. Especially then."

My hand strayed to my pocket, where the bottle of medicine pressed against my thigh. I'd been trying to quit, to be present, to face my fear instead of masking it.

I said, “I hadn’t forgotten Claridge’s.”

She looked at me blankly.

But what if the medicine wasn't just an escape, but a tool? What if it gave us both more time before the inevitable? I was defending my addiction to myself. I was scared.

"There's something else. Something I haven’t been honest about," I said. I pulled the bottle from my pocket, the cherry-red liquid catching the lamplight. "I've been... I've been using this. For years now." The confession tumbled out like bricks before a wrecking ball. "It helps with the memory, with the fog. Eight hours of clarity, of being... myself. Or a version of myself I can still recognize."

Evelyn took the bottle, turning it in her fingers. "And these past few days?"

"I've been trying to stop. To be better for you. More honest." I laughed, a hollow sound. "Ironic, isn't it? In trying to be more authentic, I ended up being less functional. Less present."

She set the bottle on the nightstand, her expression thoughtful. "Why didn't you tell me?"

"Because I was ashamed. Because I didn't want you to think that the man you fell in love with was just... a medicinal trick. Because I thought if I could just quit, just be strong enough..."

"Oh, Jesse." Her hand cupped my cheek. "You don't have to be strong alone. That's what I've been trying to tell you. We face this together—the disease, the medicine, all of it. No more secrets."

We sat in silence for a long moment, our breathing syncing, the warmth of her body against mine a tangible reminder of what we stood to lose—and what we might yet preserve.

"So," she said finally, pulling back to look at me. "A train, you said?"

I nodded, a ghost of a smile touching my lips. "I think it's time for a change of scenery. A new start, somewhere without... complications." I glanced toward the door, where Brett's intrusion had made it clear that staying at the Brunswick was no longer tenable.

"What about the Halloween celebration?" she asked, a hint of wistfulness in her voice.

"We'll celebrate on the train," I promised. "A new tradition for a new chapter."

A soft knock at the door interrupted us. Gerald stood there, his weathered face solemn but kind.

"Thought you might be needing this," he said, extending a torn piece of paper. "Found it on the floor outside of your door."

Evelyn took it, her expression softening as she recognized the Claridge's reservation slip. "Thank you, Gerald."

"Been meaning to tell you," he continued, his gaze shifting between us. I saw then, a thick orange envelope in his hand. I reached for it nervously, hoping it wouldn't be my medicine delivery at such an inopportune time. "Your past lodging expenses."

I was lost, but took the envelope and pulled it open with a thumb seeing a considerable number of pounds.

When he saw that I thought it was recompense for the altercation he said, "Greg." Then after a pause, "Told me to watch after you, and to remind you that there's a place for you both in Athens, if you've a mind to accept."

I looked at Evelyn. We'd not forgotten about Greg's invitation, the talk of circus and adventure that had seemed so tantalizing that night at the theater. I just couldn't believe he would have gone so far as this.

"Athens," Evelyn mused, a spark kindling in her green eyes. "I've never been to Greece."

"Nor I," I admitted. "Though I hear the ..."

Gerald cleared his throat. "There's a train to Paris leaves at half-ten tomorrow. From there you'd have to book a high-speed through the alps. Quite the view. I hear."

I looked to Evelyn again, seeking confirmation. She nodded, a small smile playing at the corners of her mouth. "Thank you, Gerald. That sounds wonderful."

The old man nodded, a mix of satisfaction and wistfulness in his rheumy eyes. "I'll have breakfast sent up early. Best get some rest." He turned to go, then paused. "You've been good for this old place, the both of you. Brought a bit of light to these walls. We'll miss you."

After he left, Evelyn and I sat in companionable silence, the future stretching before us like an uncharted sea. The bottle of medicine sat on the nightstand, neither hidden nor flaunted, just another reality we would face together.

"Are you sure about this?" I asked finally. "About us, about traveling together?"

She smiled. "I'm sure about the together part." Then she stood, moving to the window where the snow continued to fall in gentle flurries, perhaps getting back to the normalcy of London autumn. "I've spent my whole life either running away or being left behind," she said softly. "For once, I'd like to move toward something, with someone who sees me for who I am." She turned back to me, her silhouette limned in silver moonlight. "I am so happy to see you for who you are? It is more unique than you know."

"I still never saw my dragon."

"And I never got to Claridge's," she said, tossing the reservation in the waste basket.

I rose, crossing to her side. My arms encircled her waist.

"Whatever comes," she said to the window. "Together?"

Seeing our reflections close in the panes of glass, I said, "Always." And in that moment, it felt like a promise I could keep.

Come the following dawn, Evelyn's preparations for our departure progressed with methodical intent. As she diligently folded each garment into compact parcels, she aimed a teasing barb in my direction, marveling at the ease with which men could forsake their treasured belongings.

Yet her playful chiding found its retort in the garment bag slung across my shoulder - a humble vessel containing the few dapper accoutrements that had managed to sway Evelyn's affections. For the first time in a faded eternity, I found myself playing the role of bellhop, ferrying a lady's effects to the waiting taxi outside.

I watched her move about the room, committing each gesture, each expression to memory. This is what I feared losing most—not the grand moments or milestones, but these small, intimate scenes of domestic harmony. The way she bit her lip in concentration as she arranged her toiletries. The unconscious tuck of hair behind her ear as she bent to check under the bed for forgotten items.

I flipped through the notepad before stuffing it in my jacket pocket. The sketch of her necklace. Scrawled there was: *Memories just need good markers.* The history. A noted brand of cigarettes. Her tribal names for things like Samhain, Beltane, Alban Arthan, Oxychana. So many things…

The medicine was neither hidden in shame nor discarded. We had talked long into the night about it—its benefits and costs, the balance we might strike between dependency and clarity. In the end, she'd agreed to a compromise. I would try to rely on it less, to be present in my unaltered state as much as possible. But on days I insisted that I needed to make important decisions or hold onto precious memories, I could use it sparingly, as a tool rather than a crutch. It sounded very much like a plea an Oxy addict might make to their doctor.

After a thought, I took the pad out again and jotted: Evelyn packing—hair tuck, lip bite. Brussels Room, Oct. 28. Small anchors to tether me to this reality when the fog thickened.

As we descended the stairs for the last time, Gerald met us at the front desk, a small package in his gnarled hands.

"For the journey," he said, offering it to Evelyn. "Mrs. G's special tea cakes. To remind you of old London town."

Evelyn's eyes glistened as she accepted the gift, leaning in to press a kiss to the old man's weathered cheek. "Thank you for everything, Gerald."

Outside, the taxi driver waited, his breath fogging in the crisp morning air. I hesitated on the threshold, looking back at the Brunswick Inn one last time—the worn reception desk, the stained-glass lamp in the corner, the comfortable leather sofa where Evelyn and I had first connected over late-night conversation.

"Ready?" Evelyn asked, her hand warm in mine despite the chill.

I nodded, squeezing her fingers gently. "Together."

It was early, but we did Halloween on the train. Evelyn was lighting the candle in the ceramic pumpkin we'd purchased when I said, "The way I see it, is we should have a bout a month in Paris."

She turned the pumpkin to face me, satisfied. "That long?"

"At least that long." I thought she was mostly happy that I had scheduled a quick stop at Claridge's after all. "I was looking at the website for the circus. They've not even traveled through Hungary. They have two stops left. One in Austria and one more before their final stop in Athens."

"From what Greg was saying, it sounded as if it were permanently in Greece."

"No. According to the site, it's traveling. The schedule showed its arrival in Greece a little before—what's that grove festival around Christmas?"

"Midwinter silly."

"The proper name, I mean."

"Now my tribal voodoo is proper, then?"

I looked up from my phone and smiled.

"Alban Arthan, if you must be told again. But I should be schooling you in French instead." She came around the little table and sat beside me. Outside of the windows, hedgerows had replaced the lingering fog of the autumn plains. Evelyn lay her head on my shoulder and raised her chin at my phone. "This what you booked?"

"Yeah," I said, showing her. "The Saint-Michel."

"It looks like a hundred-year-old townhouse," she said.

"Four-hundred actually." That look she does. Then I said, "It's a bit quaint, yes. But near the station and in view of the Seine." Still the look. "I thought it might be… you know?"

"More romantic?" she asked, finally relenting.

I opened the camera app and positioned it for a selfie of us. Snapped the photo. "Absolutely."

"I suppose you might know what you're doing."

"No idea actually."

"I thought you'd been to Paris," she started saying but then stopped. "I mean, I assumed."

"Only on Google Earth. But you've been, right?"

"Was I single, or wasn't I?" Hey eyes were glued up in the signature roll.

"Huh." I was genuinely surprised. Then, leaning more into the bench seat, I said, "Go figure. First visit to the city of love, and we're both tied down."

Her eye roll broke into a smile. She said, "C'est la vie." Then, unable to judge the immense pleasure I found in her accent, she reverted back to English. "That's life," she said. "Count it as your first lesson."

Just then the train entered the Channel Tunnel, and the pumpkin took the spotlight before the fluorescents blipped on along the hall.

"As it happens, this isn't the first thing I've learned from the French," I said, moving my face close to hers.

"And how well did you learn that lesson?" She whispered, and I could feel her breath on my lips.

I had tactfully reached out for the handle of the compartment door. It clicked as I locked it.

"You be the judge."

IX. PARIS FOR TWO

We arrived at Saint Michel a little after noon, exiting RER B. Evelyn had an oversized satchel as her purse that I knew was stuffed with our toiletries, a suitcase on rollers, and a backpack. I dragged the trunk with simple rear metal casters that squeaked as it went. I also had a backpack, and a frontpack for that matter. Not to mention, my garment bag hooked on the collar of my coat.

Briefly, I wished for the convenience of a little sapient pearwood luggage with feet—something from Pratchett's Discworld that would motivate itself. It all made me wish we had just bought everything anew, but I let the thought go and stopped at the top of the steps, letting the roar of the Seine fill my ears and waiting for the small dose of syrup to catch up to me. I immediately hoped I had taken just enough because I wanted to remember this fully.

It was like stepping into a movie.

The Pont Saint-Michel bridge stretched across the river and in the distance I could see Notre-Dame's towers rising like ancient sentinels. I had let the luggage rest and stepped back before a young cyclist nearly toppled me.

"Pardon!" came the passing voice with a hand in the air.

Evelyn laughed and took my hand. "Excusez-moi!" She was waving at the youngster, her satchel falling from her shoulder and yanking our wrists, as he disappeared into the surprisingly dense crowd. It was almost like a renaissance fair. She smiled at me, reshouldering the bag, and pressed closer. That's when I could hear the violinist. All this hustle and bustle and art still shone through.

Evelyn pointed. "Over there, mon chéri!"

I could read the sign on the high-rise, though it *was* more like a townhouse with its stone façade. I looked down at the luggage and was more than relieved we were so close. Evelyn had started tugging me that way and I had to halt her to get the trunk on its casters again. Once I did, I began to notice more art. It was hiding in the false modern society. Almost as if time was trying to gobble it up, but found the spicy stuff too unappetizing to swallow.

There were many stalls, which at first looked gray and uniform, lined up in a way like those kiosks in a mall, or maybe how food trucks might park along a streetway. But as you neared each one you could sense the artistry within. The sizzle and smell of crêpes cooking. An ancient lantern burning beneath the awning of another as its owner shelved more dusty books within. Vintage prints. Street musicians. Painters.

The squeak of the casters was forgotten as we went. My senses were overcome.

The Hôtel Notre-Dame Saint Michel rose like something from a fairy tale—ivy climbing the old stone walls, wrought-iron balconies adorned with lanterns that would likely flicker to life in the evening. Through the tall windows, I caught glimpses of bold murals and rich fabrics that promised the kind of bohemian luxury I'd read about in reviews.

"Jesse, can you believe this place?" Evelyn breathed, her eyes wide as we approached the entrance. The cathedral loomed across the water, its gothic spires seeming to bless our arrival.

Inside, Christian Lacroix's theatrical design assaulted the senses in the most wonderful way. Velvet and vintage meets modern, every surface telling a story. The lobby was intimate, artistic—a lot like how Gerald had kept the Brunswick—loved, yet different from the commercial sterility of most of London.

"Monsieur Bankole," the receptionist smiled, sliding our key cards across marble inlaid with brass. "Your suite overlooks Notre-Dame. The seventh floor."

Our room was everything the lobby had promised and more. Exposed beams crossed the ceiling like the ribs of some great ship, while rich fabrics in deep burgundy and gold created an atmosphere of sensual warmth. But it was the view that stole my breath—Notre-Dame rising from the Seine like a prayer made stone, the last light of afternoon setting the water ablaze.

"Look," Evelyn whispered, pressing against the window. "It's like we're staying inside a painting."

I came up behind her, my arms encircling her waist, breathing in the scent of her hair. "Then you'll fit right in, my artist."

She leaned back against me, and I felt that familiar stirring of desire mixed with something deeper—a profound gratitude that somehow, despite all my failings and fears, this extraordinary woman had chosen to share this moment with me.

"What should we do first?" she asked, turning in my arms.

"Sleep," I said, only half-joking. The journey had exhausted us both, but the medicine was pepping me up.

She laughed, that musical sound that never failed to make my chest tighten with emotion. "We're in Paris, Jesse! We can sleep when we're dead."

And so we didn't sleep. Instead, we wandered the narrow streets of the Latin Quarter, our hands intertwined, discovering hidden cafés where accordion music drifted from shadowy corners and lovers kissed openly beneath the amber glow of street lamps.

"Look at them," Evelyn murmured as we passed a young couple pressed against the wall of a medieval church, lost in each other's embrace. "So free, so unashamed."

I studied her profile in the lamplight, noting the flush in her cheeks, the way her breathing had quickened slightly. "Does it bother you? The public displays?"

"Quite the opposite," she said, her voice dropping to a husky whisper. "There's something liberating about it. The French understand that passion is nothing to hide."

We found ourselves in a small plaza where street artists had gathered, a woman with raven hair painting portraits while a man played haunting melodies on a cello. Evelyn was transfixed, watching the artist's brush bring faces to life with bold, confident strokes.

"She's magnificent," Evelyn breathed. "Look at the way she does the shadows."

The artist glanced up, catching Evelyn's admiring gaze, and smiled. "Vous êtes artiste aussi?" You are an artist too?

"Un peu," Evelyn replied modestly, but I could hear the longing in her voice.

'A little,' I translated in my head. "Beaucoup," I said, surprising her. "And one without supplies. Perhaps tomorrow we could find you some," I suggested. "Paris has inspired artists for centuries—who knows what magic you might create here?"

Her eyes lit up with a joy so pure it made my heart ache. "Really? You wouldn't mind spending time in art shops and galleries?"

"Mind? Evelyn, watching you discover your passion is one of my greatest pleasures."

That night, as we finally returned to our room, the cathedral bells chiming midnight across the water, I asked her if she loved me and she simply said, "Beaucoup." Translation: 'A lot'.

We made love with an intensity that surprised us both. Perhaps it was the magic of the city, or the freedom that comes from being strangers in a foreign place, but every touch seemed electric, every kiss a small revelation.

Afterward, as we lay tangled in the luxurious sheets, Evelyn traced patterns on my chest with her fingertip.

"Tell me something," she said, her voice drowsy but thoughtful. "Those couples we saw tonight, so open about their desires... would you ever want to... explore that kind of freedom?"

I felt my pulse quicken. "What do you mean?"

"I don't know," she said, and I could hear the blush in her voice even in the darkness. "Maybe something like those ménage situations you read about in French novels. Not that I'm suggesting anything specific, just... curious about your thoughts."

The idea sent a bolt of unexpected arousal through me, followed immediately by a stab of possessiveness. "I think," I said carefully, "that what we have is pretty extraordinary already. But I'm not opposed to... adventure, if that's something you wanted to explore."

She was quiet for a long moment, and I wondered if I'd said the wrong thing. Then she pressed a soft kiss to my collarbone. "I love that you're open to possibilities. Most men would be threatened by the idea."

"I'm not most men," I said, tightening my arms around her. "And besides, no one could ever compare to what we have together."

The next morning brought a surprise that would alter the course of our Parisian sojourn. As we prepared to venture out for coffee and croissants, there was a knock at our door.

"Monsieur Bankole?" A uniformed DHL courier stood in the hallway, tablet in hand. "I have a delivery that required signature confirmation."

I frowned, accepting the envelope. "I did put in a change of address with DHL," I told Evelyn as she peered over my shoulder, "but I'm not expecting—you know, for days."

The envelope was thick, official-looking, with the letterhead of a law firm I didn't recognize. Inside, a cover letter explained that this was part of my father's estate, items that had been held in a safety deposit box and were only recently processed through probate.

My hands trembled slightly as I opened the smaller box within. There, nestled in velvet, was a pendant on a chain—a sun wrought in gold and silver, its rays extending in perfect symmetry. It was beautiful, ancient-looking, and somehow familiar in a way that made me forget to breathe.

"Jesse," Evelyn whispered, her hand flying to her throat where her own moon pendant rested. "Look at them together."

She held her amulet beside mine, and even in the morning light streaming through our windows, they seemed to resonate with each other, the metal warming under our touch.

"It's like they're meant to be together," I said, wonder in my voice. But even as I spoke, a chill ran down my spine. The letter mentioned my father's estate, his final effects. Estate papers usually meant...

I pushed the thought away, not ready to face what it might imply. But the weight of it settled to my feet like a stone.

Evelyn must have sensed my sudden shift in mood. "What is it, love?"

I shook my head, forcing a smile. "Nothing. Just... family history, you know? Sometimes the past has a way of catching up with you."

But I slipped the pendant over my head, feeling its weight against my chest like a promise—or perhaps a warning.

"Come on," I said, pushing away the darker thoughts. "Let's explore this beautiful city. I want to see everything through your artist's eyes."

We spent the morning wandering through the Louvre, Evelyn's excitement infectious as she pointed out techniques and influences in the masters' works. But it was when we stepped outside and she caught sight of Sainte-Chapelle's soaring spires that her expression grew wistful.

"Adam would have loved this," she said softly, her hand shading her eyes as she gazed up at the Gothic stonework. "He was fascinated by religious architecture—the way faith could inspire men to build something so transcendent. He used to say that cathedrals were humanity's way of reaching toward God with their bare hands."

I felt a familiar pang of jealousy mixed with sympathy. Adam would always be part of her story, part of what made her who she was. "Tell me about him," I said, surprising myself.

"He saw beauty in everything," she continued, her voice growing softer. "Even in war, even in loss. He taught me that art wasn't just about creating—it was about bearing witness to the sacred in everyday life."

I squeezed her hand, understanding a little better the depth of what she'd lost, and what courage it had taken for her to love again.

But it was in the medieval section that we found something unexpected—a display on Arthurian legends in French literature.

"Look at this," Evelyn said, stopping before a glass case containing illuminated manuscripts. "They have a section on the mythical artifacts—the Holy Grail, Excalibur..."

"The Thirteen Treasures of Britain," I read from the placard. "Including the Mantle of Arthur, said to render its wearer invisible, and the..." I paused, my heart skipping a beat. "The brooch of sun and moon, which could activate the mantle's power."

We stared at each other, then down at our pendants, the implications hanging heavy in the air between us.

Evelyn's face had gone pale, and I saw her swallow hard. "Jesse," she whispered, "my mother used to speak of such things. The man of the sun, the mystical union..." She trailed off, her hand unconsciously moving to her throat where the moon pendant rested.

"What is it?" I asked, concerned by the sudden fear in her eyes.

She shook her head quickly, forcing a smile. "Nothing. Just old superstitions. Tribal nonsense I thought I'd left behind." But I caught the tremor in her voice, the way her fingers had tightened around the pendant.

I'd forgotten the details of her upbringing—another memory casualty—but I could see this display had shaken something loose in her, some old fear she'd hoped to escape. "We don't have to look at this," I said gently, pushing down excitement.

"No," she said, straightening her shoulders with that determined courage I so admired. "I won't let the past control me. They're just artifacts, just stories." But even as she spoke, I noticed she kept her pendant tucked beneath her blouse for the rest of our visit.

That afternoon, we joined a tour of the Catacombs, descending into the limestone tunnels beneath the city. Our guide, an enthusiastic archaeology student named François, regaled us with tales of the underground world.

"What most people don't realize," François said as we moved through the bone-lined passages, "is that these tunnels are not unique to Paris. Recent ground-penetrating radar has revealed that similar networks exist all over the world. In Egypt, for instance, we now know that the Great Pyramid extends many kilometers underground, with chambers that may connect to tunnel systems stretching across continents."

Evelyn's hand found mine in the dim light, and I felt the pendant pulse against my chest.

"Some theorists," François continued with the kind of gleeful irreverence only the French could manage, "believe these were part of a global transportation network used by ancient civilizations. Fanciful, perhaps, but the engineering required would have been extraordinary."

As we emerged into the late afternoon sunlight, blinking like moles, Evelyn was unusually quiet.

"What are you thinking?" I asked as we found a café near the Panthéon.

"Just... what if the legends aren't entirely legend?" she said, fingering her pendant through her blouse. "What if there's more truth to these old stories than we want to admit?"

I thought of my father's journals, still waiting for me in New York, full of research I'd never had the liberty to study. "Maybe there is," I said quietly. "Maybe that's why these things found their way to us."

She never pulled out her necklace and I left it at that. It was a topic that I knew was boyish, but I could be patient. Believing in magic is one thing. But here, we had hope without it. It was good enough for me.

We spent our remaining days in Paris in a kind of golden bubble, exploring galleries and gardens, making love with increasing passion and tenderness, talking late into the night about art and dreams and the strange coincidences that had brought us together. Evelyn painted watercolors of Notre-Dame from our window, her technique growing bolder and more confident with each piece.

But beneath the surface joy, I felt the weight of something darker pressing down on me. The pendant around my neck seemed to grow heavier each day, but it wasn't just the metal—it was what it represented. Items released from probate. Estate matters. The words echoed in my mind with increasingly ominous implications.

Why would there be an estate to settle unless...?

I pushed the thought away, but it kept returning like a persistent ache. My father, alone in that nursing home, his mind already ravaged by the same disease that was slowly claiming mine. Had he finally succumbed? Had he died alone, without me there, while I'd been playing tourist across Europe?

The guilt was suffocating. Here I was, experiencing the most beautiful moments of my life with Evelyn, while my father might have been taking his last breaths, calling for a son who'd abandoned him to his fate.

"You're troubled," Evelyn said one evening as we sat by our window, Notre-Dame glowing in the twilight across the Seine.

"Just thinking," I said, not wanting to burden her with my fears.

"About your father?"

I looked at her in surprise. Sometimes her intuition was uncanny.

"The package upset you more than you're letting on," she said gently. "Estate papers usually mean..."

"I don't know," I said quickly. "I don't know anything for certain. And I'm not ready to find out." The admission felt like cowardice, but it was the truth. "What if he's gone, Evelyn? What if he died in a brief moment of clarity? And what if..." I couldn't finish the thought—what if I'm closer to that fate than I want to admit?

She moved closer, her hand finding mine. "Whatever we discover, we'll face it together. But you can't torture yourself with unknowns."

"Can't I?" I laughed bitterly. "It's what I do best." I fumbled with the lid of the little bottle of cough syrup and she put a hand on top of mine. When I looked up from it I saw meaning in her eyes. “Don’t,” they said.

She really did care. Perhaps more than I did for myself.

On our last night, as we packed for the Orient Express journey to Venice and then on to Greece, Evelyn caught me staring out at the cathedral, lost in thought.

"You're troubled again," she said, coming up behind me, her arms sliding around my waist.

"Just thinking about the future," I said, leaning back against her warmth. "About what comes after Greece."

"After Greece, we have our whole lives ahead of us," she said firmly. "Whatever shadows you're carrying from the past, Jesse, we'll face them together."

I turned in her arms, studying her face in the lamplight—the strong cheekbones, the determined set of her jaw, the eyes that held such fierce love for me despite all my failings.

"Promise me something," I said, my voice hoarse with emotion.

"Anything."

"Promise me that no matter what happens—whether we find out my father's gone, whether my condition gets worse, whether these pendants mean something we're not ready for—you'll remember this. Remember Paris, remember how we felt here."

She cupped my face in her hands, her eyes never leaving mine. "I promise, my love. But we don't have to face any of it alone."

I kissed her instead of voicing my deepest fear—that eventually, I would face it all alone, trapped in a mind that no longer recognized the people I loved most. But tonight, we had Paris, and the terrible beauty of loving someone completely while knowing it might not last forever.

Tomorrow we would board the Orient Express, beginning the final leg of our journey to whatever destiny awaited us in Greece. But tonight was ours, a perfect moment suspended in time like one of Evelyn's watercolors.

It would always be our Paris for two.

The morning after our final night in Paris brought with it a bittersweet mixture of anticipation and melancholy. As we packed our belongings in the shadow of Notre-Dame's spires, I found myself stealing glances at Evelyn, memorizing the way the light caught her hair as she folded her watercolor sketches between tissue paper.

"Ready for our next adventure?" she asked, catching my lingering gaze.

I nodded, though something in my chest tightened—a premonition I couldn't quite name. The pendant felt heavier against my skin as we made our way to Gare de l'Est.

The Venice Simplon-Orient-Express awaited us like a gleaming jewel from another era. Our Grand Suite was a masterpiece of 1920s Art Deco design, all burnished wood and crystal fixtures that caught the light like captured stars. The steward, a discreet gentleman named Philippe, welcomed us with champagne and an explanation of the suite's amenities—the marble en-suite, the double bed draped in silk, the panoramic windows that would frame our journey through the heart of Europe.

"Monsieur, Madame," Philippe said with a slight bow, "your carriage awaits."

As the train pulled away from Paris, Evelyn pressed her face to the window, watching the city recede into memory. I reached for my notepad—a habit that had become second nature—and jotted: Evelyn at window, leaving Paris. Art Deco suite. November 22nd.

The evening found us in the Lalique-panelled dining car, where Chef Jean Imbert had crafted a four-course symphony of flavors. Evelyn's eyes sparkled in the candlelight as she sampled the truffle-infused soup, and I found myself thinking how perfectly she belonged in this world of understated luxury.

"Tell me what you're thinking," she said, her fingers finding mine across the white tablecloth.

"Just... memorizing this moment," I said, and squeezed her hand. "The way you look in this light. The taste of this wine. The sound of the wheels on the tracks."

She understood. She always understood.

Later, in Bar Car 3674, a pianist played melancholy jazz while we sipped signature cocktails and watched the Burgundy vineyards roll past under moonlight. The other passengers seemed like figures from a dream—elegant couples lost in intimate conversation, solitary travelers nursing whiskeys and watching the night through rain-streaked glass.

"I feel like we're characters in someone else's story," Evelyn murmured against my shoulder.

"Maybe we are," I said, thinking of the pendant's weight, of destiny pulling us inexorably toward whatever awaited in Greece.

Morning brought the Swiss Alps, their snow-capped peaks piercing a cerulean sky. Evelyn sketched furiously as we breakfasted on French pastries and coffee, trying to capture the impossible grandeur of the Dolomites. Lake Como spread below us like a mirror, reflecting clouds and mountainsides in perfect symmetry.

"It's like the world is showing off," she laughed, holding up her watercolor of the lake.

Venice emerged from afternoon mist like a city conjured from dreams. The Santa Lucia Station received us with all the chaos and beauty of centuries. Our private water taxi cut through the Grand Canal while Evelyn gasped at every palazzo, every bridge, every impossible architectural wonder that slid past.

Our night at the Aman Venice was brief but magical—dinner on a terrace overlooking the canal, followed by champagne in a room where Byron might once have penned his verses. But it was merely a waystation, beautiful as it was.

The ferry to Greece was a different kind of luxury entirely. Our deluxe cabin featured a private balcony from which we could watch the Adriatic coastline paint itself in sunset colors. As Venice disappeared behind us, I felt that strange tightening in my chest again—as if we were crossing more than just water, as if we were crossing into something that would change us irrevocably.

"No going back now," Evelyn said softly, echoing my thoughts as she stood beside me at the rail.

The next morning brought an unexpected gift. As we breakfasted on our private balcony, watching the Ionian Sea stretch endlessly before us, Evelyn suddenly looked up from her coffee with that mischievous smile I'd come to adore.

"Do you realize what day it is?" she asked.

I paused, thinking. "Thursday, November twenty-eighth..."

"Thanksgiving," we said in unison, then burst into laughter.

The irony wasn't lost on us—two Americans celebrating gratitude while floating across the Mediterranean, bound for ancient lands and uncertain futures. The ferry's dining room couldn't offer turkey and cranberry sauce, but the Greek crew, when they learned of the American holiday, presented us with a feast of their own: roasted lamb with herbs, honey-soaked baklava, and wine that tasted of sunshine and olives.

"What are you thankful for?" Evelyn asked as we clinked glasses on our balcony, the Greek coastline a purple smudge on the horizon.

"This," I said simply, gesturing between us, to the moment, to the impossible journey we'd somehow found ourselves on. "You. Us. Even the uncertainty ahead." I paused, seeing her moon pendant dangling. My hand instinctively moving to the small bottle in my pocket—untouched now for three days since she'd stopped me that night in Paris. "And for clarity. For being present with you, really present."

She understood the deeper meaning, her eyes soft with approval. "I'm thankful for your strength," she said, reaching across to squeeze my hand. "For the way you're fighting this battle, not just for yourself but for us." Her gaze drifted to the endless blue horizon. "I'm thankful for new beginnings, for the courage to leave the past behind and step into something unknown. And..."

She hesitated, a secret smile playing at her lips.

"And?"

"For the feeling that we're exactly where we're meant to be, even if I don't understand why yet."

The words sent a strange shiver through me. My pendant pulsed against my chest again. Three days without the syrup had left my mind sharper but more fragile, like a blade honed to a dangerous edge. Every detail felt hyperreal—the salt spray on my skin, the way the light caught in Evelyn's hair, the distant cry of seabirds wheeling overhead. I was memorizing everything with desperate intensity, as if some part of me knew these moments were precious beyond measure.

She leaned across the small table and kissed me, tasting of wine and promises. "Remember Halloween on the train to Paris?" she murmured against my lips.

"Our first proper celebration together."

"And now Thanksgiving on the way to Greece. We're collecting holiday memories in moving vehicles."

I thought of time. Moving as it does. My memories likely left in the surf behind us. "What's next?" I asked. "Christmas in a hot air balloon?"

She laughed, but something in her eyes grew distant, almost prophetic. "I have a feeling Christmas is going to be... different this year."

That night, as the ferry rocked us gently toward whatever destiny awaited, I held Evelyn close and tried to burn every detail into memory—the sound of her breathing, the warmth of her skin, the way she murmured my name in her sleep, the taste of gratitude still sweet on both our tongues.

I didn't know then how precious those memories would become, how desperately I would need them in the dark days ahead. Nor did I know how the immense effort was working its magic. On my medicine it was so easy to recall, but this was a foreign practice. One I had no faith in. I only knew that I loved her with a fierce totality that frightened me, and that the pendant around my neck seemed to pulse in rhythm with the ship's engines, counting down to something I couldn't yet comprehend.

When we woke to see the Greek coastline emerging from dawn mist, purple mountains rising from wine-dark seas, I felt destiny's hand settle on my shoulder like an old friend's greeting.

Greece. At last.

X. THE GREEK HOTEL

The Greek hotel was a spectacle. Gleaming marble tiles, pristine white walls, and opulent furnishings decorated every corner. Our suite alone was massively appointed.

"Jesse, can you believe this place?" Evelyn breathed, her eyes wide as she took in our surroundings. "Look. They have a tree."

My voice was competing with the raucous of the crowd and still it threatened to get lost in the cavernous lobby. "It reminds me of Rockefeller center."

Evelyn looked at me, quizzically.

"In New York. It's an annual tree lighting ceremony back in the States."

She pointed up at the immense fir tree, festooned with glittering golden ornaments and twinkling strands of lights as I was checking in. "Oh Jesse! The angel."

I glanced over while the receptionist scribbled the room number onto the key cards and saw the exquisite porcelain tree topper, satin robes cascading under its wings. I smiled at the childlike wonder in her voice. "It's stunning."

Just off the main hallway, we discovered an intimate alcove fashioned into an inviting smoking lounge. Plush white sofas lined the shallow, secluded nook, all nestled beside an elegant spiral staircase.

"Now this is more like it," I said appreciatively, running a hand along the supple leather. "I could get used to spending my evenings here."

Evelyn hummed her agreement as she sank onto the sofa, sighing contentedly. "Pour us a drink, would you love? I have a feeling this is going to become our new favorite haunt."

During that first week leading up to the much-anticipated Globus Circus, Evelyn and I settled into the rhythms of this new culture. While she spent her days further resurrecting her passion for painting, I indulged in solitary sojourns to the lobby bar, nursing drinks while letting my mind drift. The cough syrup remained untouched in my toiletry bag—a small victory I clung to, honoring Evelyn's faith in my strength. But the scotch helped quiet the growing unease, the sense that something momentous was approaching.

No matter where our separate explorations took us, we inevitably found ourselves drawn back to our alcove haven each night like moths to a flame. The leather likely still bears the purple rings from our wine glasses.

On our fourth evening, cocooned in our smoking lounge sanctuary, we began speculating about the circus's opening night.

"Do you think we'll see Greg and the girls there?" Evelyn asked, exhaling a stream of smoke. "You should call him."

"And ruin the mystery?" I replied, swirling my whiskey. "We have time. Greg's been here for weeks, preparing that ancient coliseum of his. He'll want to be front and center, basking in the spectacle. Besides, it's divine."

"Fate, friendship," she said in the posh voices of the girls. Her eyes sparkled with anticipation. "Really, I can't wait to see them. It's been far too long since the Brunswick."

It wasn't until the fifth night, as we were settling into the plush sofas once more, that an achingly familiar peal of girlish laughter lilted down the stairs. Evelyn and I locked eyes, startled recognition passing between us—a shared déjà vu from our sojourn at the Inn. That playful siren's call proved irresistible, luring us up the spiral staircase.

The sight that greeted us stole my breath. Veronica whirled Jessica and Emily around in a blur of silken skirts and boundless joy.

"Girls, look! There they are!" Veronica exclaimed, catching sight of us over Emily's shoulder.

"Evelyn!" Emily launched herself into Evelyn's arms, the two women embracing fiercely.

I approached Jessica and Veronica. Bowing gallantly, I brushed my lips over Jessica's offered knuckles. "We couldn't mistake your voices from the smoking lounge," I explained with a wink. "Our room is just next door."

"We should have known you'd be so close," Veronica declared, swatting at my arm playfully. “You should have called!”

Evelyn eyed me playfully. It was that old sneer again. I had forgotten how much I loved it, so I sent one right back.

The hallway reverberated with the giddy thrum of our joyful reunion as breathless hellos and fervent questions ricocheted off the filigree papered walls. Veronica zeroed in on the exquisite silver amulet at Evelyn's chest, her eyes widening with keen interest.

"Darling, wherever did you find such an enchanting piece?" she inquired, reaching out a slender finger to trace the delicate metalwork.

“Yes,” I said, seizing the moment. “Wherever did it come from?”

Evelyn and I exchanged a loaded glance, entire volumes spoken in that single meeting of eyes. "It's a long story," she interjected smoothly. "One that requires refreshment and comfortable seating, I should think."

"But of course!" Veronica clapped her hands together. "Silly me, jabbering on without even a proper cocktail.

Girls, what do you say we take this scintillating tête-à-tête somewhere more conducive to catching up?"

As Jessica volunteered to scout out suitable libations and Veronica ushered a giggling Emily towards their suite for 'emergency wardrobe alterations', I pulled Evelyn aside.

"Well, this is an unexpected surprise," I murmured, caressing her cheek.

Evelyn leaned into my touch, her eyes closing for a moment. "I've missed them," she confessed. "Their energy."

"They certainly light up a room," I agreed. "Or a hallway, as it were."

Evelyn laughed, an elegant trill of mirth. Then her smile turned contemplative as she studied my face. My comment had obviously worried her. "And what about you, Jesse? How are you feeling?"

I mulled over her question, considering. I pressed my desire down again and opted to keep it relevant to our current situation. Anyway, there was a part of me that secretly relished time with Evelyn apart from the vortex of glitter and gossip that seemed to follow the trio like an entourage. But their infectious energy was hard to deny. "Truthfully? As much as I adore having you all to myself..." I grinned as she rolled her eyes indulgently. "I can't say I'm entirely displeased to be reunited with our colorful comrades. It will be nice to let loose a bit."

Evelyn nodded, satisfied. "My thoughts exactly. But responsibly. You'll let me know if…" It was a question that I had grown good at winking away. I did so again. "Now, let's not keep them waiting." Lacing her fingers with mine, she tugged me down the hall.

The night unfolded in a vivacious blur of laughter, clinking glasses, and wild tales recounted. Tucked away in Greg and the girls' lavish suite, we lost ourselves in raucous reminiscing and unbridled anticipation for the circus's impending debut.

Emily, in a daring black halter jumpsuit that Veronica assured us was fresh off an exclusive Parisian runway, perched on the edge of a plush settee as she regaled us with the trio's latest exploits. Then she and Evelyn set off together toward the powder room, their voices trailing into intimate whispers.

Sipping from a crystal coupe of Dom Perignon, Jessica nonchalantly let slip that our magnanimous host Greg also happened to own the ancient coliseum we would be gracing for opening night.

I nearly choked on my scotch. "You're joking," I sputtered, dabbing at my mouth with a monogrammed linen napkin. "Greg owns the coliseum? Plum colored Greg?"

Veronica tossed her flaxen curls over one bare shoulder, smirking. "Is it really so surprising, Darling? You have no idea the extent of that man's empire." She swanned over to the bar to refresh her Kir Royale, swaying her hips deliberately. I followed her and Jessica followed me. Then as she explained the maze of outings he'd been indulging them in, I saw Evelyn and Emily return from quite a long personal absence.

As the first blush of dawn began limning the horizon in delicate pinks and golds, we reluctantly dispersed to steal a few precious hours of sleep before the evening's grand affair. I saw Evelyn to our door, my hands lingering on her waist as I drank in her flushed cheeks and sparkling eyes.

"You enjoyed yourself," I said, more statement than question.

She smiled up at me, winding her arms around my neck. "I did. It was lovely to reconnect with them." She hesitated for a beat, searching my face. "But..."

"But?" I prompted gently, tucking a stray line of dark hair behind her ear.

"But they could never compare to you, my love," she whispered, rising up on tiptoe to brush her lips against mine. "You're my anchor, my touchstone. My port in every storm."

A wave of emotion crashed over me, so intense it stole my breath. I crushed her to me, burying my face in her hair. "I love it when you're poetic," I rasped. "You have no idea what you do to me."

She laughed shakily against my chest, her own voice thick. "I think I have some idea."

We stayed like that for suspended seconds that felt like small eternities, just holding each other, our hearts beating in synchronized tandem. The pendants at our throats thrumming with a resonance that I supposed only I could feel. Finally, I loosened my embrace and stepped back to cup her face in my palms.

"Sleep, Darling," I said softly, thumbing away the lone tear that had escaped down her cheek. "Tonight, we'll shine brighter than all the stars in the sky."

Her answering smile was a benediction, a promise. With a final searing kiss, she slipped inside our room, the latch clicking softly behind her.

I stood staring at the door for a long moment, marveling at the twists of fate that had brought this incandescent creature into my life. Then, shaking my head, I turned and made my way back down to the smoking lounge.

Sinking onto the buttery soft leather, I lit my pipe and watched the tendrils of smoke curl towards the ornate ceiling. My mind drifted to the circus and then to Evelyn's silver amulet, a tangible reminder of her strange past.

Then I thought of my own past and frowned when my father's face was more difficult to recall than it should be.

The clarity I'd maintained for days was beginning to fray at the edges. Each drink helped, but underneath the scotch's warm embrace, darker thoughts stirred and I worried I would succumb if a morning hangover proved too much. Questions about my father, about the pendant around my neck, about why I felt so drawn to seek answers I wasn't sure I wanted to find.

The anticipation for the circus had been building for days. Athens buzzed with excitement as performers arrived and vendors set up their stalls around the ancient coliseum. Greg had spared no expense in his restoration—the marble seats gleamed under strings of Edison bulbs, and the arena floor had been covered with fresh sawdust that carried the nostalgic scent of childhood memories. By evening, the air thrummed with the energy of a thousand spectators, their voices echoing off stones that had witnessed gladiators and now would host a different kind of spectacle altogether.

As the circus's opening night unfolded in a dizzying spectacle of color, music, and marvel, I found myself swept up in the grandeur, the sheer audacity of it all. Beside me, Evelyn was radiant, her face alight with wonder as she drank in every detail, from the death-defying acrobats to the snarling tigers that prowled the ring.

"Jesse, look!" she gasped, gripping my arm as a fire-dancer spun by in a whirlwind of flame. "Have you ever seen anything like it?"

The teeterboard act had me on the edge of my seat—a Romanian acrobat launched to impossible heights, landing untethered on the shoulders of a five-man stack.

I grinned down at her, relishing her infectious joy. "Never, my love. Greg certainly knows how to put on a show." But even as I spoke, a familiar unease stirred in my gut, a nagging whisper that I couldn't quite silence.

Thoughts of my father intruded, unbidden and unwelcome, his gaunt face swimming before my eyes.

I shook my head, trying to banish the specter. Tonight was about Evelyn, about drinking in the magic and wonder of this place. I wouldn't let my own demons spoil it for her.

As if on cue, Greg materialized out of the crowd, resplendent in a suit of shimmering gold silk. "Jesse, old boy!" He clapped me on the shoulder, his grin wide and white. "And the lovely Evelyn. I trust you're enjoying the festivities?"

Evelyn beamed up at him, her eyes sparkling. "It's absolutely marvelous! How do you manage all of this?"

Greg preened, adjusting his silk ascot. "Well, when one has been preparing for months, coordinating every detail..." He looked at the girls who giggled at his scorn. He trailed off with a wink. "The ancient Romans knew how to build for spectacle. I've simply awakened what was always there."

I chuckled, shaking my head. "Always so modest, Greg."

But as I bantered with Greg, my mind was miles away, spinning with thoughts of my father, of the unfinished business that hung between us like a ghost. The pendant felt heavier, as if responding to my growing unease.

Greg must have noticed my distraction, for he cocked his head, his brow furrowing. "Everything alright, Jesse? You seem a bit...preoccupied."

I pasted on a smile, waving away his concern. "Fine, fine. Just a bit overwhelmed by all this… art." I gestured to the swirling spectacle around us.

It wasn't a lie, exactly. The circus was overwhelming, a riot of sensation that threatened to sweep me away. But the tempest that truly held me captive was the rising tide of guilt and regret that I could no longer ignore. "Evelyn should be featured, she has quite a collection of paintings now."

Greg nodded, his gaze shrewd. "Is that so? It's a lot to take in." He turned to Evelyn, his smile softening. A finger went to his chin and then into the air. "Evelyn, my dear, I hate to steal you away, but I think there are some people I simply must introduce you to. Fellow patrons of the arts as it were. They would be fascinated to meet you."

Evelyn glanced up at me, her eyes wide and eager. I could see the yearning there, the hunger to immerse herself in this glittering world of beauty and creation.

A part of me wanted to hold her back, to keep her by my side as a bulwark against the darkness that threatened to consume me. But I couldn't be so selfish. Evelyn deserved this moment, this chance to shine.

I squeezed her hand, mustering a smile. "Go on, my love. Dazzle them all. I'll be right here when you get back."

Evelyn hesitated for a moment, searching my face. But whatever she saw there must have reassured her. Perhaps my many confident winks? She nodded, rising up on tiptoe to brush a kiss against my cheek. "I won't be long," she murmured. "Save a memory for me?"

I grinned, tapping her nose. "Always."

As I watched Evelyn disappear into the crowd on Greg's arm, her silvery laugh drifting back to me on the night air, I felt a pang of longing so acute it stole my breath.

What was I doing here, playing at love and lightness, when my father lay alone somewhere, perhaps entombed or cremated, the chasm between us yawning wider with every passing day? The thought was like a lead weight, an anchor dragging me down into the depths of my own misery.

I closed my eyes, taking a deep, shuddering breath and resisted the familiar urge to reach for the bottle in my jacket pocket. I'd been strong for days now, but the clarity felt brittle, like glass blown too thin.

A fanfare of trumpets shook me from my reverie, heralding the finale of the night's performance. I straightened my shoulders, reviving my false countenance as Evelyn reappeared at my side, her eyes shining with elation.

"You won't believe it! Greg says I could put my work on display."

I gathered her into my arms, breathing in the scent of her—jasmine and honey and… home. I saw my father racking his coat by the door. I could remember it still. I saw myself hooking my flat cap at the Brunswick. I had become him. Then, back to Evelyn. "I believe it," I said, rocking her and rubbing her upper arm.

The following days were a tempestuous blur, my mind a ceaseless maelstrom of warring impulses and heartrending deliberations. The allure of Greece's timeless splendors, once an intoxicating elixir, had dulled to a muted backdrop against the growing pressure in my skull.

Now, as I continued to refuse the little bottle, I became aware of missteps in my memory. Only the occasional drink helped dull the self-shame of my own shortcomings, but even that was losing its power against the mounting anxiety.

But it was Evelyn's behavior that began to gnaw at me most. She'd started spending her evenings with the girls more frequently, while I continued attending the circus for Greg's delight. She was returning later each night with stories that grew vaguer and more evasive. There was a glow about her that I'd never seen before, a secret happiness that seemed to emanate from within.

"How was your evening?" I'd ask, and she'd smile that mysterious smile.

"Wonderful," she'd say, her eyes bright but distant. "Emily showed us this little gallery tucked away in Plaka. Such beautiful pieces."

But there were other signs that made me wonder. The way she'd excuse herself to the powder room with Emily, their whispered conversations cutting off when I approached. The subtle scent of different perfumes that clung to her clothes—not her usual jasmine, but something musky and complex. Her phone buzzing with messages she'd glance at and dismiss with a secretive smile.

I tried to be sophisticated about it, tried to channel the worldly European attitude we'd discussed in Paris. After all, hadn't we talked about French openness, about the beauty of shared experiences? I told myself I should be happy that she was exploring, discovering new facets of herself.

But late at night, lying beside her as she slept with that same mysterious smile, I felt something cold and desperate clawing its way up from the depths. What if she'd found something with them that I couldn't provide? What if my attempts at clarity, my struggles with memory and medication, had left me inadequate in ways I couldn't even comprehend?

One evening, she returned particularly late, her hair slightly mussed and her lipstick gone. She moved with a dreamy contentment that made my stomach clench with something between jealousy and fear.

"Sorry I'm so late," she murmured, slipping into bed beside me. "We lost track of time."

"Doing what?" I asked, trying to keep my voice light.

She was quiet for a moment, and I could feel her choosing her words carefully. "Just... talking. About life, about experiences. You know how it is with close friends."

The way she said "experiences" sent a chill through me. I remembered our conversation in Paris about ménage situations, about the freedom that came from being strangers in a foreign place. Had she decided to explore those possibilities without me?

I lay awake long after her breathing evened out, my mind spinning with images I didn't want to see. The pendant around my neck felt like it was burning against my skin, as if responding to my turmoil and neglect.

Evelyn, ever perceptive, bore witness to my inner turmoil with a stoic grace that only amplified my burgeoning guilt. In stolen moments, her gaze would alight upon me, twin emerald beacons suffused with understanding and unconditional support. Yet even her steadfast devotion couldn't quell the rising tide of unease that threatened to engulf me.

It was during our second week in Athens that the breaking point came. Evelyn had ventured out for another evening with Emily and the girls—an endeavor that had become increasingly frequent. I'd declined under the pretext of fatigue, but in truth, I needed solitude to confront the demons that had taken up residence in my mind.

I sat in our suite with an untouched glass of amber liquor, my sole companion. Through the window, Athens sprawled before me in all its ancient glory, but I saw only the reflection of my own haunted eyes in the glass.

Hours passed. I heard Evelyn's key in the door, heard her soft footsteps as she entered. She moved with the careful grace of someone trying not to wake a sleeping partner, but I was far from sleep.

There was something different about her tonight—beyond the usual mysterious glow. She seemed slightly unsteady, one hand pressed to her stomach as if fighting nausea. Her skin had a luminous quality that could have been from passion or something else entirely.

"Jesse?" she whispered into the darkness. "Are you awake?"

I said nothing, feigning sleep, watching through slitted eyes as she moved about the room. She disappeared into the bathroom, and I heard the sound of running water, soft sounds that could have been anything.

When she finally slipped into bed beside me, she smelled different again—not just the absence of her usual perfume, but something deeper. A sweetness that seemed to emanate from her very pores.

The thought hit me like a physical blow. What if she was happier without me? What if the girls and Greg offered her something I never could—freedom from the burden of loving a broken man, experiences I was too damaged to provide?

After she fell asleep, I sat by the window, my mind spinning with doubt and self-recrimination. My father's face bloomed before my eyes, clearer now than it had been in days. James Bankole, dying. What kind of man abandoned his father? What kind of man burdened a woman like Evelyn with his failing mind and fractured memories?

And what kind of man was so inadequate that the woman he loved had to seek fulfillment elsewhere?

The bottle in my hanging jacket pocket called to me, promising eight hours of crystalline clarity. Eight hours where I could think straight, where the fog would lift and I could see my path forward with perfect lucidity.

My hands shook as I retrieved it, as I unscrewed the cap. The cherry scent rose to meet me, sweet and medicinal and familiar. I thought of Evelyn's faith in me, of her belief that I was strong enough to fight this battle.

But maybe she was wrong. Maybe what I needed wasn't strength, but clarity. Just enough to think through what came next, to make the hard decisions with a clear head.

I drank deeply—more than I'd taken in months. The syrup slid down my throat like liquid sandpaper, and within minutes, the fog began to lift. The world sharpened around me, colors becoming more vivid, thoughts crystallizing with diamond clarity.

And in that clarity, I saw the truth with devastating precision: I was a burden. A dying man clinging to a vibrant woman who deserved so much more than a future shadowed by my inevitable decline. She would stay by my side out of love and loyalty, would waste her precious years watching me fade into nothingness.

Unless I set her free.

The decision, once made, felt inevitable. I would return to America, to whatever remained of my father and my past. I would face my demons alone, as I should have done from the beginning. And Evelyn would be free to live, to love, to explore all the experiences she'd found with the girls and Greg.

With hands, steady now, with chemical clarity, I began to write.

XI. DEPARTURE

The crystal clarity was intoxicating. Every thought sharp-edged and brilliant, every solution obvious. I'd taken more than usual—much more—after days of fighting through the fog, and now my mind raced like a finely tuned engine, processing everything with perfect, chemical precision.

My hands moved across the paper with urgent purpose, the words flowing like water:

"My dearest Evelyn," I began, each letter crisp and deliberate. "By the time you read this, I will be gone. But this is not abandonment—this is necessity, love, and the clearest decision I've ever made."

The pen felt weightless in my grip as the thoughts tumbled forth, organized and logical in their manic perfection. Everything made sense now. The path forward gleamed like polished marble.

"I've realized something crucial about our journey together. You carry mysteries in that pendant of yours, secrets of your heritage that deserve proper exploration. But I've been selfish, my love, dragging you into my family's darkness when you should be discovering your own light."

I paused, taking another sip from the bottle. The syrup burned sweet and medicinal, sharpening my focus even further. Of course this was right. Of course this was the answer.

"My father's research calls to me—not just as his son, but as a man who needs to understand his own condition before it claims what's left of his mind. Five months, Evelyn. Five months to unravel the mysteries he left behind, to find treatments he may have discovered, to return to you not as a burden but as a partner worthy of your extraordinary heart."

The plan crystallized with beautiful clarity. I would solve everything. The nursing home records, the journals, whatever medical breakthroughs my father had hidden away. I would return triumphant, cured, ready to support her quest for answers about her own heritage.

"I've entrusted you to Greg's care," I continued, the words flowing effortlessly. "He will move heaven and earth to ensure your safety. And I swear to you, my love, I will return. On my birthday—May 1st—I will be waiting for you at the Brunswick Inn. From there, we can face our truths together—yours and mine—and take that ferry to the needles. Dragon or none, we might even dare venture to your homeland and face your mother as equals."

I sealed the letter with the cash and the bottle—she should understand what I'd been fighting, what I was trying to conquer for us both. The concierge took the envelope with professional discretion, and I felt the weight of decision settle into my bones like warm honey.

This was right. This was noble. This was the action of a man who loved completely and thought clearly.

As the taxi carried me through the Athens night toward the airport, the city lights streaked past like falling stars. I closed my eyes and surrendered to the chemical confidence coursing through my veins, already planning my triumphant return.

I had no way of knowing that by morning, when the syrup's false clarity faded and the crushing weight of what I'd done settled in, I would be halfway across the Atlantic, too proud and too ashamed to turn back.

XII. THE ACHING PAST

The flight back to the States was a blur of restless dreams and crushing sobriety. As the aircraft charted its course across the Atlantic, the crystal clarity that had driven me from Athens began to fracture, leaving behind jagged shards of regret and a throbbing headache that pulsed in time with the engines.

By the time we touched down at JFK, the chemical confidence had evaporated entirely, replaced by the familiar fog and a nausea that had nothing to do with turbulence. I stopped at the airport bar for some relief and sat, the guilt plaguing me while I scheduled the cab ride to my old post office.

The weight of what I'd done—leaving Evelyn, abandoning our future for this selfish quest—threatened to entomb me in shame. So, I had another drink.

The post office box on Twenty-Second Street was crammed with the detritus of my absent years. Box twenty-two—I'd purchased it when I turned twenty-two, the same year I'd finally accepted I would never know my mother. Now, as I sorted through the mail with trembling fingers, that number seemed to mock me with its persistence. Bills, advertisements, notices—and there, among the refuse, envelopes bearing the blue sword and shield of Belleview Nursing Home. My hands shook as I sorted through them, the progression telling its own grim story: discharge papers, transfer notifications, and finally, the thin manila envelope that contained everything that remained of my father.

"Spring Creek Memory Care," I read aloud to the taxi driver, my voice barely audible over the engine. The building sat squat and utilitarian under the cone of an orange security light, its double doors as unwelcoming as a mausoleum.

The receptionist's face told me everything before she even opened the file. She'd been saving the obituary, she explained, rubber-banding it with his medical records and a small envelope that chilled me to see.

"I'm responsible for the clipping," she said gently. "I thought if someone ever came..."

There it was in black and white: James Bankole, 67, survived by one son. The dates blurred together as I stared at the page. He'd been gone for months while I'd been discovering myself in London, falling in love in Paris, playing at adventure in Greece.

But it was the small envelope that made me start—inside, a silver key and a deed to the apartment on Lake Fern and Elm. Twenty-two.

Back in the cab, I sat turning the silver key over in my hand as the sleet began to stick to the window. I breathed onto the glass, watching the fog form and fade. The silence stretched between us until I finally spoke.

"You know where Lake Fern crosses Elm? East side?"

The cabby glanced at me in the rearview mirror, his eyes crinkling. "Yeah, sure do. Used ta wrestle around in Compton Pahk when I was a kid. Right neah theah."

I nodded, tracing patterns in the condensation on the window. Something about his easy familiarity with the neighborhood made my chest tighten. This stranger knew my childhood streets better than I did anymore.

"Small world," I managed.

"Dat it is, buddy. Dat it is." He paused, studying my face in the mirror. "You got a pahticular address, or you just want me ta drop ya at da cornah?"

I looked down at the deed in my hands, at the numbers that seemed to follow me everywhere. The same number that had marked every milestone in my fractured life. "Twenty-two Lake Fern," I said quietly.

"Twenty-two, huh?" The cabby's voice softened slightly, as if he'd heard something in my tone. "Goin' home?"

The question hung in the air between us. Twenty-two years old when I'd stopped believing in family. Twenty-two dollars left in my pocket the day I'd aged out of the boys' home. And now, twenty-two Lake Fern—the address I'd never known belonged to us.

"Something like that," I said.

The rest of the ride passed in comfortable silence, the cabby seeming to understand that I needed the quiet. As we pulled up to the brownstone, he turned to look at me fully.

"Take cayah of yahself, son," he said, and there was something in his voice—a gentleness that made me think he'd driven this route before, had carried other lost souls back to places that were no longer quite home. As I fumbled for bills with numb fingers, the nursing home paperwork still clutched in my other hand, he added softly, "Merry Christmas, buddy. Hope things look up for ya."

The brownstone looked smaller than I remembered, shabbier, like a photograph left too long in sunlight. The key turned easily in the lock, as if the apartment had been waiting for my return.

Inside, dust motes danced in the thin shafts of light that filtered through drawn curtains. And there, by the door, stood the coat rack—mahogany and brass, just as I remembered. I could see my father hanging his overcoat there after work, could see myself as a boy reaching up to hook my school jacket on the lower peg.

I touched the wood reverently, feeling the grain beneath my fingertips. Some memories, at least, remained vivid.

The office was exactly as he'd left it. The steel safe squatted beneath his desk like a sleeping beast, and I fumbled for the combination he'd hidden in his final letter. Twenty-two-twenty-two, I read from the page—even in death, he'd used the number that had shaped my life, as if he'd known I'd need that familiar constant to guide me through the darkness he'd left behind.

Inside lay the remnants of a life's obsession: yellowed journals, faded photographs, and research that made my blood run cold.

The first journal opened to a hand-drawn map of the Congo Basin, marked with careful notations in my father's precise script. But it was the sketch on the facing page that stopped my heart—a crescent moon pendant, rendered in loving detail, every curve and whorl captured with the devotion of a man in love.

"The amulet," the caption read. "The key to the ancient mysteries. Without its twin, it remains dormant, beautiful but powerless."

I turned the page with trembling fingers. More sketches, more notes. References to "the twin brooches of Camelot," to Arthur and Morgan's tragic bond, to the power that could only be awakened when sun and moon were reunited. My father had been researching the same legends I'd stumbled into, following the same myths that had led me to Evelyn.

A photograph slipped from the journal. I lifted it trembling. Looked away and back again. "What the?" I was looking at Evelyn! But it couldn't be! But there she was, radiant, the moon pendant gleaming at her throat. On the back, in my father's handwriting: "The love of my life. Mother of my son."

I stared at the words, the syrup making them shimmer and dance on the page. Mother of my son. Not sons. Not children. Just... son.

My hands were already turning pages, seeking more, finding entries that painted a picture I didn't want to see.

A loose piece of paper fluttered from between the pages—a simple note in my father's handwriting: "Research partner still owes outstanding debt. Will honor agreement when needed." Nothing more. I crumpled it and tossed it aside, my mind too consumed with the revelation about Evelyn to care about my father's business dealings.

"Mohami bore me a son," my father had written in careful script. "A child of fire, imbued with the moon's mystery. Alas, the tribe's laws are clear—only daughters can inherit the sacred knowledge. A son is... expendable."

The words blurred as understanding crept in like poison.

This was a photo of Mohami! But Evelyn...

I flipped frantically through more pages, finding a more detailed map, notes about tribal customs, and then—there—a passage that threw me into a strange and terrifying trip:

"She will have other children, Mohami says. The next will be a daughter, she is certain. The moon's bloodline will continue through her, while my son grows up safe in America, never knowing the burden of his birthright."

My vision began to shake as if I were stuck in some electric field.

Half-sister.

The revelation hit like a sledgehammer to my chemically amplified consciousness. Not twins separated at birth, but siblings born years apart to the same mother, by different fathers. Evelyn, the sacred daughter raised in the ways of the tribe. And I, the disposable son shipped off to obscurity.

I read on. "Arthur and Morgan's curse lives on, generation after generation. These can only be musings of a sick man losing his mind."

I doubled over, the room spinning like a carnival ride. The syrup made every sensation hyperreal—the taste of bile in my throat, the sound of my own ragged breathing, the smell of dust and old paper that seemed to carry the weight of family secrets.

We'd found each other. Across continents and cultures, through pure chance or cosmic design, we'd found each other and fallen in love with the passion that only shared blood could explain. The attraction, the instant connection, the feeling that we'd known each other forever—it all made horrible, perfect sense.

A sound escaped me then—half sob, half laugh—that echoed in the small room like something breaking. I pressed my palms against my temples, trying to hold my skull together, trying to process what this meant for us, for what we'd shared, for the future I'd promised her.

The research scattered around me told the whole sordid story. My father's obsession with the ancient myths, his discovery that the legends were real, his horror at realizing what bloodlines could create when they converged. And us, Evelyn and I, playing out the same tragic script, dancing to the same cursed music that had doomed Arthur and Morgan centuries before.

I grabbed another journal, tearing through pages with manic intensity. There had to be more, had to be some way out of this nightmare. But every entry only confirmed what I already knew, each revelation driving the knife deeper into my chemically enhanced consciousness.

"Separated him at birth," one entry read. "Gave the boy to the adoption agency, prayed distance would break the cycle. Thought an ocean would be enough. Thought time would erase what blood had written."

But blood doesn't lie. Blood calls to blood. And we'd found each other, drawn together by forces older than civilization itself.

I was laughing again, or maybe crying—the syrup made it hard to tell the difference. Everything was connected, everything was planned, everything was wrong. The pendant around my neck burned against my skin like a brand, marking me as half of a broken whole.

The bottle called to me from my jacket pocket, promising relief from this enhanced agony. But even as I reached for it, I feared it! I knew it might spiral me into oblivion. Nothing would help. Nothing could change what we were, what we'd done, what we'd felt in each other's arms.

Half-sister.

The words tasted like ash and medicine, like childhood dreams curdling into adult nightmares.

As the chemical haze settled over my thoughts, another realization crept in like a cold draft. My father's early Alzheimer's, his rapid decline, the way he'd seemed to retreat from the world in his final years—what if it hadn't been the disease at all? What if he'd been drowning his guilt the same way I was now, medicating himself into forgetfulness rather than face what he'd set in motion?

I thought of the nursing home receptionist's words: "He was always asking for medicine, something for the anxiety, something for the pain." Not physical pain—the pain of knowing. The agony of watching his son grow up ignorant of the truth that would one day destroy him.

Had my father spent his last years in this same chemical fog, chasing clarity that only brought more horror? Had he looked at my face and seen Mohami's eyes, Evelyn's mouth, the ghost of a love that had damned us all?

The bottle gleamed in the harsh motel light, offering its familiar promise of eight hours without memory, eight hours without pain. It dared me to push through. I stared at it, understanding with perfect, terrible clarity that I was about to make the same choice he had. But understanding didn't equal strength. Knowledge didn't grant salvation.

My hand closed around the bottle's neck, and I drank deeply, tasting my father's despair in every drop.

For how could I face her, knowing what I now knew? How could I hold her in my arms, knowing that the blood that flowed through our veins was the same cursed ichor that had damned us both from the moment of our birth?

As I pondered these things, the cold rain pelted my face and mingled with the hot tears that streamed down my cheeks. How could I possibly stop thinking of Evelyn as I walked the slippery streets of the Big Apple alone?

XIII. EVELYN'S RETURN HOME

"I'm with child."

Evelyn knew it before she pulled open the accordion-style leather envelope Jesse had left behind. Though they'd been careful in their lovemaking since Paris, that first passionate night had been deep, unguarded love without regrets or doubts. She'd expected something from him—his recent discomfort had revealed that much—but she never expected him to disappear entirely.

She understood his desire to close the chapter on his father. She had her own need for closure, and she thumbed the silver moon amulet when she thought of it. But why the complete estrangement? She wanted to be there for him, with him.

The three girls pampered and loved her as if she had always been their partner, and Greg watched over her with genuine care. But she would have rather been with Jesse. Still, as the five months passed—the date he had marked for his return—she found herself growing stronger, more independent. The weight of the life growing inside her made her feel powerful rather than fragile.

Calls had gone unanswered. An excess of WhatsApp messages were left on read. The only message she hadn't sent was the one she knew would send him running back immediately. She made a line with her fingers right below her navel and decided against it. If Jesse needed time to sort out his family demons, then she would handle her own.

Greg traveled with her to London during the final week, and there they waited in the familiar atmosphere of the Brunswick Inn.

"Been mighty quiet 'round here without the girls," Gerald said to Greg one evening as they sat smoking in the lobby. Evelyn ignored their exchange, twirling the vape she had substituted for cigarettes absently between her fingers, watching the spring rain streak the windows as a couple entered through the front doors.

A week after Jesse's promised date had passed, Greg and Evelyn found themselves at the old tavern down the road when a saxophonist began singing in French. Evelyn recognized the song and asked Greg to dance, singing the words softly as they turned, the solitary couple on the floor.

"Such a lovely language," said Greg, dropping a few pounds into the open instrument case.

"I'm a bit rusty," said Evelyn, though she felt more confident in French now than she had in years.

"So what now?" Greg watched her pick up the glass of weak wine. "It's been a week. Maybe you should tell him about the baby."

She took the rest of the drink and placed it back thoughtfully on the table. She looked up at him with a new resolve. "No."

Greg flinched at her firmness.

"You know," she said, settling back in her chair, "I first heard that song at a dive in Nigeria, after I had just set out on my own from the base. Mohammed drove me to the city, introduced me to a man who could help sell my artwork. I didn't really need the money—I had Adam's pension and hardly indulged in much of anything at that point. But I was building my own life."

"Sorry, darling. Mohammed?"

"General Mohammed. After my first husband died in the war, I stayed on the base for a while, but it became clear that I couldn't live there indefinitely. The war was over, and they'd be moving on. So they helped me get acclimated to society." She paused, a new confidence in her voice. "I made my own way then, and I can do it again."

"You know you can stay with us, Evelyn. Jesse told me to watch out for you and we are—"

"No," she said firmly. "I could have gone home after Adam died, but I was scared of what my mother might say. I was a child then." Her hand moved to her belly. "I'm not a child anymore."

The saxophone keyed up a few warm-up notes again and Greg looked that way. When the music started, he looked back at Evelyn expectantly, but something had shifted in his expression—a weight she'd never seen before.

"Are you saying you want to go home?"

"I'm saying I want answers. About my heritage, about this pendant, about the things my mother never told me." She lifted her chin with determination. "Jesse is dealing with his father's legacy. Maybe it's time I dealt with mine."

Greg was quiet for a long moment, his fingers drumming against his glass. When he spoke, his voice carried an unusual gravity. "Your father's legacy, you mean."

Something in his tone made Evelyn look at him sharply. "What do you mean?"

Greg seemed to wrestle with himself before continuing. "Evelyn... there are things about your family's past, about Jesse's father's research, that you should know before you make this journey."

"What kind of things?"

"The kind that explain why I've been so invested in keeping you both safe." Greg's usual theatrical air had vanished entirely. "Your father—your real father—wasn't just some passing adventurer who charmed your mother and disappeared. He was a researcher, an academic. And he wasn't alone in his work."

Evelyn felt the pendant grow warm against her skin. "Greg, what are you saying?"

"I'm saying that when you go back to your people, you need to understand that there are forces at play—people who have been waiting for this moment for decades. People who knew James Bankole, and who know exactly what that pendant around your neck represents."

The weight of his words settled over her like a shroud. "You knew him. Jesse's father."

Greg nodded slowly. "We were... colleagues. Partners, in a way. And I made him a promise before he died—a promise that's kept me watching over his son ever since."

"What kind of promise?"

"The kind a man makes when he knows he's unleashed something dangerous into the world." Greg's eyes were distant now, haunted. "James discovered things in that jungle, Evelyn. Ancient things. Powerful things. And he paid a price for that knowledge that's still being collected."

Evelyn's hand instinctively moved to her pendant. "This has something to do with the artifacts, doesn't it? The sun and moon."

"Everything," Greg said simply. "Your mother, your bloodline, Jesse's condition—it's all connected. James knew it, and it destroyed him. But he also knew that one day, the pieces would come together again. And when they did..."

"What?"

"Someone would need to be there to make sure the right choice was made." Greg met her eyes. "That someone is me, Evelyn. It's why I've orchestrated so much of what's happened. The circus, the travels, bringing you two together—none of it was coincidence."

The revelation hit her like a physical blow. Everything—their meeting, their journey, even Greg's presence in their lives—had been guided by forces she was only beginning to understand.

"So when I go home," she said slowly, "you'll come with me not just as a friend, but as..."

"As someone who owes a debt to your father. And to you." Greg's voice was firm now, resolved. "We can take the Hyperloop through France and into Spain. It's only a three-hour trip. From there we'd have to fly into Kisangani and rent a Range Rover."

Her eyes brightened with anticipation rather than apprehension, but now tinged with new understanding.

"There's a layover in Nigeria, and a pretty nice place I can hold up in Kisangani after I drop you off at the village.

You know I need certain amenities." He pulled up his shirt cuffs and gave her a pert wave, but the gesture felt different now—less frivolous, more protective. "Someone there should be able to guide you if the path has changed."

"You would go with me?" she asked, touched by his loyalty but now understanding its deeper roots.

"It's a two-day journey, but yeah, darling," he stirred his coffee. "Jesse would have my neck if I let you go alone. Besides," he grinned, and for a moment his old theatrical self returned, "James made me promise to see this through to the end. Whatever that might be."

She gave him a knowing look and put a hand on her belly. "Yes. I certainly know."

The following morning brought new purpose. As they prepared for the journey, Greg handed her a small wrapped package.

"What is this?"

"Something James asked me to make copies of for his child when the time came. I wasn't sure if it would be Jesse or..." He gestured to her pendant. "But I think it's meant for you."

Inside was a small leather journal, filled with careful reproductions of James's handwriting. Maps, sketches, and most prominently, detailed drawings of the very pendant she wore.

"He knew," she breathed. "He knew what would happen."

"He suspected. And he prepared as best he could." Greg's voice was gentle. "The journal will help you understand what you're walking into, Evelyn. Your mother's people aren't just guardians of old stories—they're the keepers of something much more significant."

Being back in Africa was euphoric for Evelyn, but now tinged with new understanding. Her Parisian French came back easily, though she found herself having to adjust to the colonial French and local pidgin that mixed through the conversations in Kisangani. She was translating between multiple dialects now, which felt natural rather than frustrating—like rediscovering a skill she'd always possessed.

Since leaving Kisangani, the road had been nothing but a single lane of broken blacktop that snaked under a couple of interstate bridges before dropping completely into the Congo Basin.

"Thank you, Greg," she said, watching the familiar landscape roll past, but now seeing it through different eyes—not just as homecoming, but as destiny.

He nodded, keeping focused on the madly curving road.

"I do hope Jesse is okay," she said. "I fear what he'll do when he discovers that James has passed. He may not handle it well." She paused, realizing the truth of it. "I need to do this for myself. For my child. And now I understand—for my father's memory as well."

Greg glanced at her through the corner of his eye, both hands on the wheel. "You're different, you know. Stronger."

She smiled, one hand on her belly, the other clutching James's journal. "I've had to be."

When the reflective orange of a street sign reading "Njaran Village" appeared fastened to one of the wider roots of a banyan tree they drove through like a cave, Evelyn felt not just excitement, but a profound sense of completing a circle that had begun long before her birth.

The village had evolved since her childhood memories—children playing between homes that showed signs of modern adaptation, solar panels catching sunlight, PVC pipes bringing clean water. This wasn't the primitive isolation she'd fled from as a teenager. This was a community that had adapted while maintaining its roots.

When Evelyn saw a young woman stand up amid a garden of vine-ripe tomatoes and wipe her hands, she felt not just ease, but recognition. This was progress, evolution—her people had found a way to bridge old and new.

The Land Rover came to a stop and residents began to approach—cautiously but peacefully. Evelyn leaned over and kissed Greg on the mouth, a gesture of gratitude that now carried the weight of deeper understanding.

"You're not going to get any reception out here, but you have the two-way radio. Save the battery. I'll be back here in three days. Are you sure you don't want me to hang around for a while?"

Evelyn got out and had a brief exchange with two young girls in a mixture of French and what she remembered of the local dialect. Greg could make out the word "Oxychana" and saw the girls' eyes light up with recognition and respect—but also something else. Wariness, perhaps. Or anticipation.

"It's about an hour's walk from here, following the old trading path. Things have changed, but I'll be fine." She waved the radio at him confidently, but now her confidence was tempered with knowledge. "They're traders now, Greg. They deal with the outside world. But they're also the guardians of something much older."

"Just be careful, girl."

"Hey," Evelyn said, catching the faint smell of Oxychana sage burning from the village, "they're like family. And I'm not the scared girl who ran away anymore. I'm James Bankole's daughter, coming home to claim my heritage."

As she walked away, Greg watched her go with a mixture of pride and profound worry. He'd kept his promise to James this far—now came the hardest part. Letting her face her destiny alone, while praying that the path James had set in motion so many years ago would lead to salvation rather than destruction.

In her pack, James's journal seemed to pulse with its own weight, carrying secrets that would soon reshape everything she thought she knew about her family, her people, and the true power of the pendant that hung around her neck.

Here, the villagers worked together, living by different means than anything in London or Nigeria. The community was much closer-knit because it had to be. They shared their homes and kept busy with daily duties. It wasn't exactly foreign to Evelyn, just a long lost memory which she was doing her best to rekindle. She tried getting in the mindset of the women.

A trio of teenage Njaran girls offered Evelyn a roof for the night but she refused, longing to close the distance to her tribe by nightfall. She had seen bundles of the dried Oxychana on the porches of the homes and it had been explained that they had been trading with the tribe for things like pvc pipe, and plastic jugs. Their woven baskets and many of their vegetables came from her mother's gardens. So her mother still managed the commerce! Two of the village ladies agreed to be her guide and a child had been sent ahead to alert the village of their party.

The old grading machines that had leveled the military base loomed above her as they crossed into the jungle. She realized they must have dug down to the clay to make water run off from the site, because when she looked back from under the trees, it was like staring out from a magic mirror onto a city construction site, never finished. But now that they had walked the soggy wooden plank, which served to make an easier transition from the rubble of the site to the floor of the jungle, Evelyn was immersed in her past.

The trail opened up to a well-worn path one would have missed if not directed by the locals. Thin metal posts held a low rope that drooped its way along either side of the walkway. She was surprised that copper lamps accented well-placed wooden poles every hundred yards or so, and they were not alone for the entirety of the trek. Twice, they came upon a couple walking in their direction, bound with baskets and sacks, no doubt headed back to the Njaran slum. And then the kid who had brought the message on his return trip. But the most euphoric thing Evelyn encountered on the trail was something that stirred deep childhood memories---it was the Dolmen. She remembered her mother bringing her here as a young girl for tribal ceremonies, the ancient stones both terrifying and fascinating to her child's mind.

The Dolmen hidden behind fronds. It was chained off much like an exhibit. The dark abyss that was its interior could be made out from under the lip of polished rock that somehow tricked the eyes into thinking it was nothing but a dome. There was a cavern there; Evelyn knew it, saw it, felt it. Much like a picture puzzle that tricks the mind until one finally realizes they can see a pretty young lady and a crone by simply shifting their perception, the Dolmen spoke to Evelyn. Yes, she could see this cavern, the trick the eyes were playing on her mind, and the way the stone of the Dolmen gently helped its deceit. The moon around her neck grew hot. Then, before she could ask about it, the woman beside her pointed out the plaque by the wayside. Etched into the bronze was a cryptic sort of message.

Who but I can know the secrets of the unhewn dolmen?

Who but I can reveal the mysteries of the moon?

Who but I can find the secret resting place of the sun?

"What does it mean?" she asked, the woman.

The woman only made a motion toward the locked gate, directing Evelyn's gaze back to the stone monolith. Then the other woman put a hand on her shoulder. "The Ba'Aka people believe it guards the mantle of Arthur. Do you know this name?"

Evelyn thought back to what her mother had taught her, then remembered Jesse's passion, but falsely shook her head as if at a loss.

"The Pygmies believe the British king and his Druid Merddin left behind relics that lie dormant here."

"You mean King Arthur?" Jesse's boyish little adventure. She almost laughed.

"You do know?"

"Well, Britain is thousands of miles from here. I've spent my time in London where it is a popular story."

"Not so far when the seas were gathered in one place," the woman said, moving slowly away and continuing down the trail.

Evelyn glanced back over her shoulder at the dark entrance beneath the stone, but it had been an illusion. Then she noticed that fruits were growing abundantly along the trails edge, and the smell of Oxychana already had begun welcoming Evelyn in its embrace. The closer they came the more Evelyn accepted that she would be here regardless of Jesse's actions, for she had told herself many years ago, when she loved Adam, that if she were to bear a child, she would return.

As Evelyn and her companions drew closer to the heart of the Oxychana village, the scent of the sacred herb grew stronger, permeating the air with its heady fragrance. The trail widened, and the sounds of life—the laughter of children, the rhythmic pounding of pestles, and the distant chanting of the elders—began to filter through the dense foliage.

Evelyn's heart raced with anticipation, each step bringing her closer to the place she had once called home. Memories flooded her mind, images of her childhood spent exploring the lush jungle and learning the ancient ways of her people at her mother's knee. She recalled the long nights spent in the sacred hut, inhaling the sweet smoke of the Oxychana and allowing her mind to soar on the wings of the ancestors.

But amidst the excitement, a flicker of uncertainty took root in Evelyn's heart. She had been gone for so long, had lived a life so different from the one she had been born into. Would her people still accept her? Would they understand the choices she had made and the path she had taken?

As if sensing her thoughts, the Njaran woman turned and said, "The messenger child reported that they are waiting for you." Her voice filled with reverence. "The whole village will gather to welcome you home."

Evelyn felt tears prick at the corners of her eyes, overwhelmed by the love and acceptance radiating from the woman's words. She nodded, not trusting herself to speak, and allowed her to lead her forward, through the final stretch of the jungle and into the clearing that housed the Oxychana village.

The sight that greeted her stole the breath from her lungs. The village was just as she remembered it, a sprawling collection of huts and communal spaces arranged in a circular pattern around the central fire pit. But it was the people who caught and held her attention—faces, young and old, all turned towards her with expressions of joy and reverence.

At the center of the gathering stood a figure Evelyn would have recognized anywhere, even after all the years that had passed. Mohami, her mother, the great priestess of the Oxychana, stood proud, her dark eyes glittering with unshed tears.

"My daughter," Mohami said, her voice ringing out vibrant and strong across the clearing. "You have returned to us at last."

Evelyn felt her own tears spill over as she rushed forward, closing the distance between them in a few swift strides. She fell into her mother's embrace, breathing in the familiar scent of herbs and woodsmoke that clung to her skin.

"Mother," Evelyn whispered, her voice muffled against Mohami's shoulder. "I'm so sorry. I never meant to be gone for so long."

Mohami pulled back, cupping Evelyn's face in her hands and searching her eyes with a gaze that seemed to pierce straight through to her soul. "You have nothing to apologize for, my child," she said softly. "You followed the path the ancestors laid out for you, just as we all must do."

Evelyn nodded, fresh tears coursing down her cheeks. She knew her mother spoke the truth, but the guilt and uncertainty still lingered, a weight she could not easily shed.

As if reading her thoughts, Mohami's gaze drifted down to Evelyn's swollen belly, and a knowing smile curved her lips. "And now you have returned to us, bearing the future of our people within you," she said, her voice filled with wonder and reverence.

Evelyn placed a hand on her stomach, feeling the life that grew there, the child that had been conceived in love and hope. "Yes," she said softly. "But the father…"

Mohami shook her head, silencing Evelyn's words with a gentle touch. "The father's path is his own," she said firmly. "But you, my daughter, have a destiny that has been written in the stars since the beginning of time. And we, your people, will be with you every step of the way."

Two villagers stepped aside and a handsomely chiseled man of Africa emerged from behind them.

Serat was not in the cut-off shorts and tee she remembered, but wore only a quilt-like burka, which revealed his powerful thighs and left the glistening muscles of his chest bare. A string of tree nuts was over his shoulder and his grin was a perfect white crescent. His sparkling eyes did nothing to hide his awe of her beautiful glow.

She didn't know they hid another thing, for the silver flash of the moon amulet had already crossed his vision.

Evelyn reached out for him, her kiss landing squarely on his mouth.

She almost thought he had embellished, but then quickly, he held her at arms length and laughed heartily. "Look at you! You're beautiful. How I have missed the sight of you. How do you feel?"

"A bit weary, but you!" She hugged him again then stepped back. "You're handsome, and a man. I mean. Well, you've been eating!" Then they both laughed.

The villagers gathered around, their faces alight with joy and anticipation.

"He has become quite the hunter," said Mohami as they began walking. "And educated, too. Many nights I have to pull him from the totem houses after dark."

Evelyn felt a sense of peace settling over her. She knew the road ahead would not be easy, that there were secrets and challenges she had yet to face. But here, in the heart of the Oxychana, surrounded by the love and wisdom of her people, she had a different strength.

With a deep breath, Evelyn allowed herself to be led forward, into the waiting arms of her tribe. The ancient rituals and sacred rites of the Oxychana called to her, a siren song she could no longer resist. And as the drumbeats began to rise and the scent of the sacred herb filled the air, Evelyn began to think that she may have to accept that this was home.

XIV. THE FLIGHT

Thoughts of oceans of purple hue touched by pinkish cloudy skies rode with Evelyn as she sat with her mother in the dugout bowl of her abode. The snug little hut that her mother now had to herself was packed with purple pillows and lacy things that she adored. A tiny, tiled kitchenette had been built here with ready water from the spring, brought along through PVC, where their house had stood so long ago.

It was a modern, cleanly-kept lodge within, set right out in the middle of the hidden village. The other villagers had houses which were built in much the same fashion, but none of them were this luxurious. Straw and dry palm roofing cones still prevailed, but more prominent building material was in the walls.

It was nearing nightfall and the people had mostly returned to their homes, candle-lamps burning among the welcoming sounds of the surrounding forest and comforting night-cap of the canopy. It was different, but it was home. Any feelings of reservations were slowly fading with the aroma and ever-present smoke of the Oxychana.

"I see that the practices have not changed?" Evelyn said.

"Nor have our beliefs," said Mohami, smoking the dried herb they knew too well. "Have yours?"

Evelyn felt a tinge of guilt and when she remained silent, her mother dismissed it. "It has been lonely since your father's departure," said she.

"Off on another adventure?"

"This is different," said her mother. "I've stopped counting the years. We've moved on."

Evelyn could see her weighing the reaction.

After a tense moment, Evelyn sighed, then reached out in an automatic fashion taking one of the small rolled quids from her mother's tray and tucking it into her cheek.

"I shouldn't have left," she said as the leaf softened between her teeth and gums. Then she began to tell her mother of the night she left and her tricking Serat. She told her of the military base and of Adam.

It was when she was telling of their marriage when her mom held up a hand to quiet her.

"Elithis was not your father," Mohami said simply.

The words hit Evelyn like a physical blow, even though she'd suspected it from Greg's careful revelations during their journey to Africa, had pieced together the truth during those quiet moments when he'd spoken of James Bankole and forces that had been waiting. But hearing it spoken aloud, confirmed by her mother's own lips, made her heart lurch against her ribs. The potent sour liquid of the bundled roll of leaf was already seeping into the sensitive porous flesh of her gums, making her thoughts swim at the edges.

James Bankole, she thought, the name Greg had spoken with such weight and knowledge. My real father. But she forced her expression to remain neutral, let her mother see only the shock she expected to see.

Mohami continued explaining the reason for Elithis's lengthy absences in her youth—how he had brought the suitors, how the deception had been maintained. When she saw Evelyn becoming impatient she said, "Your birth father was a suitor." Before Evelyn could demand more, she continued. "You didn't get the opportunity to grow close with your grandmother. She died when you were young. But she also was a seeker. The practice is forbidden of being committed to writ. It is for that reason we formed the cellars."

Evelyn thought back. "I wasn't schooled in the totem writing, but I remember father, I mean, Elithis, walking me along the lines of leaves by candlelight, and showing me the intricate symbols. He told me we could read them by flipping through one by one."

"You would have soon been taught," said Mohami, who then took another draw from her pipe. When she released the smoke she said, "Each leaf has a burned symbol into it representing a syllable. Only in that way could our teachings be retained without violating the religious law."

Her mother never faltered, only sat with glassy eyes that looked reminiscent of old, as she began to reveal the truth about Evelyn's real father—or at least, the version of truth she wanted to tell.

The fluids from the pack of herb were now thick in her cheek and Evelyn felt the onset of the trance lightly threatening. She reached into her gums and hooked the mashy substance from her mouth with two fingers, hoping to stop the effects from taking hold. She slung it to the ground, resisting an urge to confront her mother with what she really knew, but it was too late.

The flight had begun. Any moment she knew she would be standing along those seas of purple with her mom, and there would be nowhere to run. But perhaps, Evelyn realized with a clarity that cut through the drug's haze, there was nowhere she needed to run. She had knowledge now that her mother didn't know she possessed. She could use that.

"I see it is taking you," her mother said. "Stay calm my daughter, there are things you need to know to ensure the direction of the flight."

Evelyn tried to relax, but her mind was working even as the Oxychana pulled her deeper. She erected a mental barrier around Jesse's image, around the truth of James's research, around everything she'd learned from the journal. If her mother wanted to control this narrative, to shape Evelyn's understanding of her heritage, then Evelyn would let her—for now. But she would remain aware, would filter every revelation through what she already knew to be true.

Mohami summoned the question that had moved Evelyn to flee as a young woman. It was drawn from her and came from her mom's lips in that old unique way. "Did you not ask yourself the same thing I asked myself before the pact that was our upbringing?"

Evelyn looked to her, her mind sharpening for a moment in pure intent, even as the drug clouded her thoughts. "Who is the man of the Sun? And how would I know?"

The question came from Evelyn as perfect melody sings from the clarinet of a woodwind master. It was there, in this moment that her mother leaned in to embrace her, whispering through the silken hair that hung as a curtain before her ear.

"After I was pregnant with his first child, we had secret meetings in the forest. Outside of the dolmen. He was a white man. Anglo-saxon heritage, from America. Like you, I questioned if I could make the choice while under the influence of the Oxychana leaf."

James, Evelyn thought, the pieces falling into place exactly as Greg had hinted they would. But she kept her face carefully neutral, let her mother believe she was hearing this for the first time.

Mohami had taken Evelyn's upper arms in her hands and their eyes were directly across from one another's. "This man was my father?"

"Yes." Her mother said softly. "He stayed for a year and a day until his son was weaned. Your brother, born first. Then, just before his departure..." She paused, her eyes growing distant. "He left me with you, though he never knew."

Brother. The word hit Evelyn like lightning, and suddenly Greg's voice echoed in her memory: "I wasn't sure if it would be Jesse or..." He had trailed off, gesturing to her pendant, but now she understood what he'd almost said. Jesse or... her. Both of them James's children. Both of them...

Her mind reeled as the pieces crashed together. Greg had known. He'd almost told her, but she'd been too focused on learning about James being her father to catch the full implication. Now the truth was unavoidable: the man she loved, the father of her unborn child, was her older brother.

She was succumbing to the flight and yet her mother's eyes still held firm. Then before her mother let her fall comfortably back against the abundant softness of those purple pillows, Evelyn heard herself say, "Jesse... Jesse is my brother?"

The words escaped before she could stop them, genuine horror overriding her careful control. This revelation cut deeper than anything else—not just that James was her father, but that Jesse, her Jesse, was her older brother. The man who had protected her, loved her, given her this child growing within her womb.

Then she could do nothing more but listen, and dream, as her mother's words came alive, twisting and dancing among paisley colored drifts of wind and smoke.

Her mother's words then whirled as she received them, each word a cliff on which to hang and each phrase a moral in itself. She listened as Mohami told of the horror of being taken by her next suitor, Elithis, after knowing she was already full with babe. The way she loved Elithis in a different way than she had held James.

"When you disappeared and Serat came hurrying to my hut, I knew that you had found the one. It was with a heavy heart that we managed our way to the very spot you'd disappeared. You were gone. I feel it is his babe you carry now within you. Like mother, like daughter ..."

But she was wrong. It was not Adam's baby at all. And Jesse was her brother—her older brother—and the child she carried was born of their forbidden union. The weight of that knowledge pressed down on her even as the drug tried to lift her consciousness away.

Evelyn felt the thought spiral through her mind as the Oxychana took full hold, but somewhere in the depths of her consciousness, the horrible truth remained, waiting like a coiled serpent for the moment when she would need to face what they had done, what she was carrying, what their love had created in innocence and would birth in knowledge of sin.

With those words, the old lady settled back herself, flying to her daughter who would be waiting on the shores of Pangea.

Standing on the shores of Pangea in the dream state of the Oxychana was something Evelyn had not done since she was but a teenager. Now she stood alongside her mother, not as her pupil, but as her equal. And they gazed out across the seas, from which stories said they had come. Now, Evelyn knew not what to believe. She remembered the story of man's creation from the Bible, and found it lovely. She fancied the way that the first couple had lived in perfect union and stood naked with no shame.

In this state of mind, there were no problems. She could hear the thoughts of her mother just as clearly as if she had watched the words purse from her lips themselves. She could see her mother's intent on raising her child another Seeker. The thought occurred to her within these mists of vivid dreams. Instead of terror, she felt an unsettling logic in the idea, but her mature mind knew it was directly influenced by the sage.

In that knowledge she strengthened her mental barrier, blocking out Jesse's visage more carefully now.

The new knowledge of their potential blood relation made protecting that secret even more crucial. She always thought of her mother as supernaturally cunning, a notable strength, but Evelyn would take advantage of the single weakness she still possessed—her vanity. And though the flight was entirely one-sided, as she held her mother's hand and listened to the thoughts come through, rising above breaking waves, she let her assume that she'd been told everything.

But Evelyn held back the most dangerous truth of all—that she already knew who her brother was, had already loved him as more than a brother should be loved, was already carrying his child. The man who had left her in Greece, searching for answers about his father, was the very brother her mother spoke of. In the dreamscape, she felt her mother's satisfaction at having shared the family secrets, unaware that her daughter possessed the most damning knowledge of all—that the ancient taboos had already been broken, that the bloodline had already been tangled beyond redemption.

Together they drifted as a downy feather in the wind, up and over the lush forest with its emerald foliage and lucid burning fruits of red. They rose higher as if they were an eagle catching the spiraling updraft in its massive wings. Above the Super Continent, they flew inward toward its center, past a massive volcano, dwarfed only by the great pyramid. Their winged souls lifting on warm torrents of steamy thermals and circling above the gaping maw of smoldering magma within, they rushed upward in the pure white steam that was their Mother Earth's first breath of life.

When Evelyn made out patterns in the smoky whiteness of the flight, she knew that she was coming to. She let it come back to her at its leisure. When her eyes once again regained some focus and her skin picked up on the gentle strokes of chilly paint that was being applied to her; she breathed in deeply as if trying to regain possession of her soul from the very air around her.

The scents of the hut reminded her instantly of where she was, the sandalwood and myrrh, and, of course, the Oxychana. She was safe but still in the paralyzing and heavy grasp of the herb. With a great effort she dropped her left hand from the arm of the wicker chair in which she had been placed (while she was unconscious, she guessed) to the slight roundness of her belly, which now was being decorated in the spiral of the invocation. The warmth of the life within her permeated the skin of her tummy and moved into her hand, and her lip trembled into a smile.

But beneath that smile, her mind was racing. Jesse was her older brother—born first, weaned before she was even conceived. The man she had fallen in love with, the father of her child, was the son James had written about in his journals. And the innocent life growing inside her—their child—was the product of a love that nature itself had forbidden.

The paint spirals on her belly suddenly felt like brands, like the markings of some cosmic punishment for sins committed in ignorance. She was no longer just a woman carrying a child; she was a sister carrying her brother's offspring, a living testament to the cruelest twist of fate.

From her fixed gaze, she saw her mom working at the fireplace, which had been mortared up with stone, a small chimney breaching the lofty rooftop. A cauldron hung within the interior and fresh spices were orderly atop the table to the left. When Evelyn noticed the blue flecks of paint along her mom's forearms she understood it as a sure sign of the fertility festival and wondered who she was being prepared for.

The question took on new urgency now. If Serat believed he was destined to be her mate, if her mother was preparing her for some sacred union, then her knowledge of Jesse—of their blood connection, of the child already growing within her—became not just personal revelation but potential weapon. The fertility ritual seemed obscene now, a mockery when she was already carrying the forbidden fruit of her brother's love.

For now, she would play the role her mother expected: the prodigal daughter, returned and ready to fulfill her destiny. But Evelyn was no longer the frightened girl who had fled the village years ago. She was a woman with the most terrible secret of all—she had already committed the ultimate transgression, had already borne the consequence of loving her own blood. The child within her was proof of that impossible love, and no amount of ritual paint or sacred ceremonies could undo what had been done in innocence and would now be lived in knowledge.

The paint continued to dry on her skin as she planned her next move.

XV. THE REVEREND'S BURDEN

The apartment on Lake Fern had become a tomb. Empty bottles of Robitussin DM littered the coffee table alongside takeout containers growing new species of mold. Johnny Walker bottles—some empty, some half-full—stood like amber sentinels among the scattered pages of my father's journals. I hadn't opened the curtains in weeks.

The mahogany coat rack by the door held only my father's old overcoat, dust motes dancing in what little light filtered through the grimy windows. My own clothes lay wherever I'd shed them, the apartment's order dissolving along with my grip on reality.

Three months. Three months since Christmas Eve, since I'd opened that safe and learned the truth that shattered everything I thought I knew about love, about family.

The journals lay open around me like tarot cards spelling out doom. Mohami's photograph smiled up from the coffee table, her face so achingly similar to Evelyn's that sometimes, in my chemical haze, I forgot which was which. The maps of the Congo Basin had become my obsession, the carefully drawn symbols seeming to pulse with meaning just beyond my comprehension.

I reached for another bottle—my tolerance had grown frightening—and drained half of it in one pull. The world sharpened around the edges, thoughts crystallizing with that familiar artificial clarity that had become both salvation and curse.

The pendant around my neck grew warm against my skin. My father's sun, waiting for its moon.

I'd promised to meet Evelyn on my birthday. May 1st. Seven weeks away, and I still didn't know if I was strong enough to face her, to look into those green eyes knowing what we'd done in ignorance.

Children of the same blood, bound by more than love.

The thought sent me stumbling toward the door, my father's journals clutched against my chest like a shield. I needed guidance, needed someone to tell me that the connections spinning through my mind weren't just the ravings of a broken man drowning in cough syrup and guilt.

St. Bartholomew's loomed ahead through the March sleet, its spires piercing the gray sky like accusing fingers.

"Forgive me, Father, for I have sinned," I began, the words tumbling out in a familiar rush. This was my fifteenth visit to Reverend Williams in the past month, each confession more desperate than the last.

"Jesse," the reverend's voice carried deep concern now. He'd watched my deterioration week by week, visit by visit. "My son, perhaps we should speak face to face today—"

"No!" The word exploded from me. "You still don't understand what I've discovered. Everything connects, Father. Everything!" I pressed my father's journals against the confessional screen, pages crackling. "The Tower of Babel, the Congo tribes, Arthurian legend—it's all the same story repeating across time!"

"Jesse, you're speaking very rapidly again. When did you last eat? Sleep?"

I laughed, the sound harsh in the small space. "Sleep? Father, I've been having biblical revelations! Do you know what I found in my father's research? We're all related—every single human being descended from the same source. Adam and Eve, Noah's family, one blood scattered across the earth!"

"That's... that's a theological interpretation, yes, but—"

"Not interpretation! Fact!" I took another long pull from the bottle in my coat pocket, feeling the medicine sing through my veins. "And you know what that means? It means what I've done—what Evelyn and I have done—it's not unique. It's the original pattern, the template written into our very DNA!"

Silence stretched between us. When Reverend Williams spoke again, his voice was barely a whisper. "Jesse, what exactly are you saying you've done?"

The confession poured out like poison from a lanced wound. I told him about Evelyn, about our meeting, our journey across Europe. About the love that had bloomed between us and the terrible discovery hidden in my father's journals.

"She's my half-sister, Father. Same mother, different fathers, but the same cursed bloodline. We fell in love not knowing, lay together, and now..." I pressed my face against the screen. "Now I understand why God scattered the tribes at Babel. Not out of anger, but out of mercy. To prevent exactly what Evelyn and I have done."

"Jesse, listen to me very carefully—"

"But here's what haunts me!" I interrupted, my voice rising to near-hysteria. "Tell me about the Tower of Babel, Father. Tell me why God really knocked it down!"

The reverend cleared his throat nervously. "According to Genesis, humanity spoke one language and came together to build a great tower to reach heaven. But God saw their pride and scattered them, confusing their tongues and spreading them across the earth—"

"Yes! Exactly!" I could feel the syrup and alcohol mixing in my system, creating a cocktail of clarity and madness. "One people, one blood, one language! Before God divided them, they were united! Just like my father's research shows—the original continent, Pangea, when all the lands were one and all the peoples were one family!"

"Jesse, I'm very concerned about your mental state—"

"Don't you see?" I was on my feet now, pacing the tiny confessional. "The Oxychana remember! Evelyn's people, they use sacred herbs to see visions of when the world was whole, when the continents were joined. It's all in my father's notes! And the artifacts, Father—the sun and moon pendants that can supposedly reunite what was divided..."

I pulled out the pendant, holding it up to catch the dim light filtering through the screen. It seemed to pulse with its own inner fire.

"What if the Tower is meant to rise again? What if Evelyn and I, what if our child, is part of some cosmic plan to heal the divisions that God created? What if the bloodlines mixing isn't a sin but a necessity?"

"Jesse, these are dangerous thoughts—"

"Are they?" I pressed closer to the screen. "My mother—my real mother—is still alive in the Congo. She knew my father, bore his children, and if the research is right, if the bloodlines really do carry the power to reunite what was scattered... Maybe I need to go there. Maybe I need to find her and learn the truth about what we really are!"

"Jesse, you absolutely cannot travel to Africa in this condition—"

"I have to!" The words came out as a roar. "Don't you understand? May 1st—that's my birthday, that's when I promised to meet Evelyn. But how can I face her without knowing the truth? God knows I want to be with her again! But how can I without understanding whether we've committed the ultimate sin or fulfilled the ultimate destiny?"

I was crying now, tears and snot streaming down my face. "Maybe the Tower needs to fall again before it can rise properly. Maybe some bloodlines need to be purified in the fires of their own making. Maybe—"

"That's enough." Reverend Williams' voice cut through my rambling with sudden authority. "Jesse, I want you to stay right here. Don't move. I'm calling for help."

"No!" I grabbed for the confessional door. "I have to go! I have to find the truth before—"

But I could already hear him on his phone in the adjacent booth, his voice urgent: "Yes, this is Reverend Williams at St. Bartholomew's. I have a parishioner here who's having what appears to be a severe psychiatric episode. He's talking about international travel, he's clearly intoxicated, and I believe he may be a danger to himself..."

I stumbled out into the church proper, the pendant burning against my chest and my father's journals scattered across the floor. The reverend emerged from his booth, phone still pressed to his ear, his face etched with genuine concern and fear.

"Jesse, please. Let us help you."

But I was already moving toward the exit, my mind racing with plans and possibilities. Flights to catch, a mother to find, a truth to uncover that might just save us all—or damn us completely.

Three days later, I stood in JFK's international terminal with a one-way ticket to Kinshasa clutched in my shaking hand. The intervening time was a blur of frantic planning and chemical courage. I'd booked the flight online, packed my father's research, and consumed enough cough syrup to maintain the crystalline clarity that made everything seem possible.

The gate agent looked at my ticket, then at my appearance—unshaven, eyes bloodshot, clothes that hadn't been changed in days. "Sir, are you traveling for business or pleasure?"

"Family," I said, the word feeling strange on my tongue. "I'm going to meet my mother."

Something in my voice must have concerned her, because she flagged a supervisor. Soon I was surrounded by airline security, airport police, and a TSA agent who kept asking to see my identification.

"Mr. Bankole," one of the officers said, "we've had a report that you might be in distress. Can you tell us why you're traveling to the Democratic Republic of Congo?"

I tried to explain—about my father's research, about the Oxychana tribe, about the need to understand my heritage before I could face my future. But the words came out in a rush, connections that seemed crystal clear to me sounding like gibberish to their ears.

When they found the multiple empty bottles of cough syrup in my carry-on, along with a remaining one of my father's journals covered in what they probably saw as obsessive scribbling, the decision was made.

The psychiatric hold was swift and efficient. As they led me away from the gate, I caught a glimpse of the departure board: my flight to Kinshasa, boarding in thirty minutes, a connection to a truth I might never now discover.

"Wait!" I called out, struggling against the gentle but firm hands guiding me toward the medical facility. "You don't understand! I have to be there! I promised her I'd return on my birthday!"

But they were already calling Bellevue, already processing me into the system that would keep me safe from myself and the world safe from whatever madness they saw burning in my eyes.

The last thing I remember before the sedative took hold was the pendant around my neck, still warm against my skin, still waiting for its moon.

The psychiatric ward at Bellevue smelled of industrial disinfectant and broken dreams. They'd brought me in raving about biblical genealogy and ancient towers, my blood alcohol content dangerously high, my system flooded with enough dextromethorphan to kill a horse. The 72-hour hold became a week, then two, then a month as my body fought to purge itself of the chemical cocktail I'd been living on.

"Mr. Bankole," Dr. Martinez said during our first coherent session, her voice professionally kind but firm. "You've been placed on extended psychiatric hold. The combination of substances in your system could have killed you. Can you tell me what you remember about trying to board that flight?"

I sat in the sterile room, hands trembling as the last of the cough syrup worked its way out of my system. The artificial clarity was gone, leaving behind a gray fog that made everything feel distant and wrong. "I was trying to find my mother," I said quietly.

"Your mother lives in the Congo?"

"She's part of a tribe called the Oxychana. My father did research there in the 1980s." Even saying it out loud, it sounded less urgent somehow, less cosmically important than it had felt in the confessional. "I found his journals. There were... connections I needed to understand."

Dr. Martinez made careful notes. "And you felt you needed to travel there immediately?"

The date hit me like a physical blow. "May 1st. I promised someone I'd meet them. In London. On my birthday." I looked at the calendar on her desk—March 30th. "How long have I been here?"

"Five days. But Mr. Bankole, I need you to understand something very serious. You were found with massive amounts of dextromethorphan in your system—that's what's in cough syrup. Have you been using it regularly?"

Shame flooded through me. "It helps with my memory. I have early-onset Alzheimer's, and the DXM gives me clarity for a few hours. Makes the fog lift."

"I see. And how long have you been self-medicating this way?"

"Years," I admitted. "But lately, since I found my father's journals, I've been taking more. Much more."

Over the following weeks, they stabilized me on lithium and selegiline—medications that Dr. Martinez explained would help regulate my mood and slow the cognitive decline. But there was a price.

"These medications are MAOIs—monoamine oxidase inhibitors," she said seriously during our third week. "They're very effective, but I need you to understand something critical. These drugs cannot be mixed with dextromethorphan under any circumstances.

The interaction can cause serotonin syndrome, which can be fatal. More relevant to your condition, it can cause severe cognitive disruption, hallucinations, even complete temporary amnesia."

I nodded, feeling clearer than I had in months. The lithium had dampened the manic urgency that had driven me to the airport, but it had also swept away the chemical fog. I could think again, remember clearly—including the devastating truth about Evelyn and what we'd unknowingly done.

"There's something else," I said during our session in mid-April. "The person I was supposed to meet. Her name is Evelyn. She was... my bed partner."

Dr. Martinez leaned forward with interest. "And she's expecting you on your birthday?"

"May 1st. We agreed to meet at a hotel in London." I stared at the calendar on her wall, watching the days tick by with agonizing slowness. "She's probably already there, waiting."

"Have you tried to contact her?"

I shook my head. "I can't. Not until I understand what we are to each other. What I learned in my father's journals... it changes everything."

"Would you like to tell me about it?"

The whole story came pouring out—meeting Evelyn, our journey across Europe, the love that had grown between us, and finally the terrible discovery that we shared the same mother. Dr. Martinez listened without judgment, occasionally asking clarifying questions, never once showing the horror or disgust I'd expected.

"That must be incredibly difficult to process," she said when I finished. "No wonder you felt compelled to seek answers."

"She was waiting for me," I said, my voice breaking. "Is waiting for me. And instead of being there to support her through her pregnancy, to face this together, I'm locked up in here because I couldn't handle the truth."

Dr. Martinez consulted her notes. "Mr. Bankole, your response to trauma is understandable, but the way you were coping—the substance abuse, the manic behavior—that wasn't sustainable. You could have died."

April bled into May with excruciating slowness. I attended group therapy sessions, took my medications without complaint, spoke calmly about my "break from reality" and my commitment to seeking proper treatment. The doctors were pleased with my progress, but they weren't ready to release me yet.

On May 1st—my birthday—I sat in the common room staring at the wall clock as if I could will time to reverse itself. Somewhere across the Atlantic, Evelyn was probably sitting in the Brunswick Inn's lobby, watching the door, waiting for a man who would never come.

"Happy birthday, Jesse," said Marcus, my roommate, a gentle schizophrenic who collected bottle caps and spoke to angels. "You look like someone died."

"Someone did," I said quietly. "The man she fell in love with. The man who promised to be there."

I imagined her waiting through the afternoon, through the evening, finally accepting that I wasn't coming. Would she understand? Would she hate me? Would she assume I'd simply abandoned her?

The guilt was a living thing gnawing at my insides. Every day that passed made it worse, made the possibility of ever explaining myself seem more remote. How do you tell someone you love that you missed the most important day of both your lives because you'd discovered you were siblings and had a complete psychological breakdown?

By mid-May, I'd perfected the art of appearing stable. I spoke rationally about my condition, expressed appropriate gratitude for the care I was receiving, and demonstrated insight into my previous behavior. The doctors began discussing discharge plans.

"You've made remarkable progress," Dr. Martinez said during our final session. "But I want to make sure you understand the importance of continuing your medication and avoiding any substances that could interact with it."

"I understand completely," I said, and I did understand. I also understood that the moment I walked out those doors, I was going to find the nearest pharmacy.

"You mentioned wanting to travel to learn about your heritage. I think that's a healthy goal, but perhaps you should wait a few months, get fully stabilized—"

"Of course," I agreed readily. "I need to focus on my recovery first."

The lie came easily. I'd learned to tell them what they wanted to hear, to project the image of a man who'd learned from his mistakes. Inside, the need to find answers burned as bright as ever. Brighter, even, fed by weeks of guilt and the knowledge that I'd already lost Evelyn through my cowardice.

They released me on May 18th with a supply of lithium and selegeline, a list of outpatient resources, and stern warnings about avoiding alcohol and over-the-counter medications. I nodded seriously, shook Dr. Martinez's hand, and walked out into the spring sunshine a free man.

The first pharmacy I found was six blocks away.

The bottle of Robitussin DM felt familiar in my hands, like greeting an old friend who'd led you astray before but promised better times ahead. I knew what Dr. Martinez had said about drug interactions, knew the risks, but I also knew I couldn't face what came next without chemical courage.

I drank half the bottle in the pharmacy parking lot.

The effect was immediate and terrifying. Instead of the familiar crystalline clarity, my thoughts became a kaleidoscope of fragmented images. The lithium and selegeline, still circulating in my bloodstream, created a toxic symphony with the DXM. Reality warped and shifted around the edges, faces in the crowd becoming my father's, then Evelyn's, then dissolving into abstract patterns of light and shadow.

But through the chaos, one thought remained constant: I had to find the truth. About the Oxychana, about my mother, about whether the love Evelyn and I shared was a sin or part of some larger design. I'd missed our reunion, failed her when she needed me most. The least I could do was arm myself with answers before I crawled back to her, begging forgiveness.

At JFK, I bought another ticket to Kinshasa with hands that shook only slightly. The pendant around my neck pulsed with warmth, and my father's research—somchow preserved through my hospitalization in my personal effects—seemed to glow with possibility.

The airport was different this time. No concerned gate agents, no psychiatric evaluations. I was just another traveler with a valid passport and a destination. The chemical fog in my brain made everything feel dreamlike, unreal, but it also provided a strange confidence. I was no longer the desperate man who'd been dragged away from this same terminal two months ago. I was a seeker, a researcher, following in my father's footsteps toward a truth that might justify everything.

As the plane lifted off from New York, I took another careful sip from the small bottle in my jacket pocket. The city fell away beneath me, and with it, the last vestiges of the man I'd been before I learned the terrible truth about blood and love and the weight of genetic destiny.

Below us, somewhere in London, Evelyn was probably still waiting, still hoping, and wondering where I'd gone.

Soon, I told myself through the chemical haze, I'd have answers. Soon, I'd understand enough to go back to her with something more than apologies. Soon, the pieces would fall into place, and the love we'd found in ignorance might be transformed into something deeper, something that could survive the truth of what we were.

The plane banked east, toward Africa, toward the Congo, toward a mother I'd never known and secrets that might damn or redeem us all.

Twenty hours later, I would stumble off that plane in Kinshasa with no clear memory of the journey, my mind a battlefield between conflicting medications and the growing urgency of a quest I could no longer fully articulate. But the pendant would still be warm against my chest, and my father's map would still point the way to a village hidden in the heart of the jungle, where a woman named Mohami waited with her own terrible truths about the children she'd loved and lost.

XVI. THE PROMISE

The village materialized from the jungle like something from a fever dream. My father's map had led me here through two days of stumbling through dense undergrowth, the pendant around my neck growing warmer with each step. The chemical cocktail in my system—lithium, selegeline, and whatever remained of the cough syrup I'd consumed on the plane—made everything shimmer at the edges, reality bending like heat waves.

Children scattered at my approach, their eyes wide as they took in my disheveled appearance. My expensive jogging suit was torn and mud-stained, my face unshaven, my eyes wild with the particular madness that comes from mixing prescription drugs with street medicine and desperation.

An older woman emerged from one of the huts, speaking rapidly in a language I didn't understand. She gestured toward a man approaching from the center of the village—tall, powerfully built, with the confident stride of someone accustomed to authority.

"You are lost, brother?" the man asked in accented English, his voice warm with genuine concern.

I fumbled for the map, my hands shaking. "I'm looking for the Oxychana. My father... he had research...

I need to understand..." The words came out in fragments, my thoughts scattered by the drugs and exhaustion.

The man smiled, a flash of perfect white teeth. "I am Serat. And you have found us." He studied my face with curious eyes. "Come. You look tired, hungry. We will talk."

"Serat?" I looked up sharply, recognition cutting through the sluggishness of withdrawal. "Evelyn told me about you."

Something shifted in his expression—surprise, perhaps calculation, but it passed so quickly I might have imagined it. "Evelyn spoke of me?" His voice was carefully neutral. "It has been many years since I heard that name."

He led me to a small hut on the outskirts of the village, gesturing for me to sit on woven mats that covered the earthen floor. The space was intimate, masculine—hunting weapons on the walls, carved totems in the corners, the lingering scent of herbs and woodsmoke.

"You have traveled far," Serat observed, settling across from me. "From America, yes? I can hear it in your voice."

I nodded, still clutching the map. "My father... James Bankole. He came here, years ago. He left me this." I held up the pendant, and Serat's eyes fixed on it with an intensity that seemed almost hungry, though his expression remained carefully neutral.

"Your father left you well-equipped for your journey," he said, his gaze lingering on the amulet for a moment longer before meeting my eyes again. He reached into a leather pouch and withdrew a collection of dried herbs, his movements practiced and ritual. "But first, we smoke. It is our way of welcoming visitors, of opening the mind to truth."

The Oxychana burned with a sweet, cloying smoke that filled my lungs and sent tendrils of warmth through my already compromised system. Whatever psychiatric medications were still circulating in my blood seemed to amplify the herb's effects, making the walls of the hut pulse with their own heartbeat.

"Better," Serat said, watching as the tension left my shoulders. His fingers drummed against his knee as his eyes drifted back to the pendant at my throat. "Now we can speak as brothers." He leaned back, his posture relaxed, inviting confidence. "Tell me, what brings you to our sacred lands? And how do you know of Evelyn?"

The story poured out of me—my father's death, the journals, the terrible discovery about my heritage. But it was when I explained my relationship with Evelyn that Serat's attention truly sharpened.

"Evelyn, she lives?" he said, his eyes widening with what looked like genuine surprise.

My heart sank slightly. "So you haven't seen her? She's been gone that long?"

Serat's expression grew wistful. "Not since she ran away, many years ago. But brother, I have known Evelyn since we were children. She and I..." He gestured vaguely, his smile turning nostalgic. "We grew up together, climbed the same trees, swam in the same streams. Such a beautiful girl, even then. Wild as the jungle cats, with eyes like emeralds and a spirit that could not be tamed."

The Oxychana made everything feel hyperreal, every word Serat spoke painted in vivid colors. I found myself leaning forward, hungry for details about the woman I loved.

"She told me about this place," I said. "About the traditions, the sacred sites. About you."

"Did she?" Serat's eyes glittered with amusement, though something flickered across his face—recognition, perhaps, or calculation. "What did she say about old Serat?"

"That you were... important to her. That you cared for her."

Serat nodded slowly, his expression growing thoughtful. "I did care for her. More than she perhaps realized." He took another draw from the pipe, studying me through the smoke while his gaze kept returning to the pendant. "But Evelyn was always meant for greater things than village life. She had to follow her path, seek her destiny beyond our borders."

"She's in London now," I said, the words slightly slurred. "Waiting for me to return. I promised myself I'd find answers about my past, about what we are to each other, before we could be together properly."

Something definitely flickered in Serat's eyes now—too quick for me to catch in my altered state, but unmistakably present. "Ah, yes. The eternal questions. Who are we? Where do we come from? What is our purpose?" He leaned forward conspiratorially. "Tell me, brother, what did you discover in your father's journals?"

I found myself spilling everything—the maps, the tribal connections, the truth about Evelyn being my half-sister. In my drugged state, it all seemed like an adventure, a quest for ancient wisdom rather than the nightmare it had been in New York.

Serat listened without judgment, nodding at intervals, occasionally asking clarifying questions. His fingers continued their unconscious drumming, his eyes occasionally flicking to the pendant as if working through some internal puzzle. When I finished, he sat in contemplative silence for several minutes.

"A powerful story," he said finally. "The bloodlines converging, the ancient patterns repeating themselves. Your father was a wise man to document these things."

"But what does it mean?" I asked desperately. "What are Evelyn and I supposed to do with this knowledge?"

Serat smiled, but there was something different about it now—a hint of calculation I was too impaired to recognize. "Evelyn always was clever, that one. She knew you would need to understand your heritage before you could move forward together."

"She did?"

"Of course. A woman like Evelyn, she needs a man who knows himself completely. She tricked me once, you know—disappeared into the night when I thought I had her figured out." He chuckled, shaking his head. "You must not let her slip away so easily, brother. She respects strength, wisdom, a man who seeks truth about himself."

The Oxychana had made me euphoric, filled with possibility. "Yes! That's exactly what I need to do. Find the truth, understand what I really am, then return to her with wisdom."

"Precisely." Serat's voice was warm, encouraging. "And fortunately for you, brother, the answers you seek are closer than you think."

"They are?"

"The dolmen. The ancient stone circle where your father first met Evelyn's mother. It holds the secrets of your bloodline, the truth of what you and Evelyn represent." He leaned closer, his voice dropping to an intimate whisper, his eyes bright with something I mistook for friendship. "The sacred site remembers everything—every union, every child born of ancient power. If you truly wish to understand your destiny, you must go there."

My heart was racing now, whether from the drugs or excitement, I couldn't tell. "Will you take me there?"

Serat shook his head. "This is a journey you must make alone. It is the way of the ancestors—only in solitude can you hear their voices clearly." He reached into his pouch and withdrew an old brass key. "But I can give you this. It will open the way."

I took the key with trembling fingers, feeling its weight, its age. "How will I find it?"

"Follow the old trading path, past the village boundaries. The dolmen calls to those who carry the blood—your inheritance will guide you." His gaze lingered meaningfully on the pendant one more time. "Go there, learn what you need to know, then return to London with the wisdom Evelyn deserves. Show her you are a man worthy of her love."

The idea filled me with intoxicating purpose. Here was the answer I'd been seeking, the way to transform the curse of our bloodline into something sacred. I could return to Evelyn not as a broken man fleeing from truth, but as someone who understood the cosmic forces that had brought us together.

"Yes," I breathed. "Yes, that's perfect. She'll understand then. We both will."

Serat smiled and nodded approvingly. We smoked in companionable silence for several more minutes, two men bonded by shared appreciation for an extraordinary woman and the ancient mysteries that surrounded her.

My mind lapsed momentarily, a strange vision clouding out all else. I saw a purple sea and a volcano looming in the distance. Then I began to rise and thought for a moment I had succumbed to sleep but the man shook me and pointed to the door.

As I prepared to leave, checking that I had the key and my father's map, Serat stood and walked with me to the exit. He paused.

"One more thing," he said casually, his eyes dropping to my feet. "Your shoes."

XVII. SERAT

Serat descended the worn stone steps, the flickering torchlight casting eerie shadows on the damp walls of the cellar. The air hung heavy with the scent of earth and secrets, the weight of ancient knowledge pressing down like a physical presence. He moved with the grace of a predator, his footsteps echoing in the stillness, the only sound the distant drip of water and the rasp of his own breath.

He had walked these paths countless times, had traced the lines of the Ogham leaves until their shapes were seared into his memory. But tonight, with the sun amulet so close at hand and the prophecy trembling on the cusp of fulfillment, the cellar felt different, charged with a palpable energy that made his skin prickle and his heart race.

Serat paused before the towering racks of preserved leaves, their surfaces glistening in the dancing light. He reached out with trembling fingers, tracing the delicate whorls and spirals, feeling the thrum of power that emanated from each one. These were the sacred texts of the Oxychana, the repository of their history, their beliefs, their very identity.

And at the center of it all, the prophecy.

The leaves spoke clearly: both pendants were required. The sun and moon, united, would unlock the dolmen's deepest secrets. But Serat smiled as he read the ancient warnings. No one had ever succeeded in opening the sacred site. Not in living memory, not in the stories passed down through generations. The dolmen remained sealed, impenetrable, its mysteries locked away from mortal eyes.

The outsider—Jesse—would find nothing but stone and frustration. He would stand before the ancient monument with his precious amulet, would fumble with the key, would grow angry and confused when nothing happened. Then he would return, defeated, ready to listen to reason.

Serat's fingers drummed against the leaf's surface as he calculated. The ceremony first—claim Evelyn as his mate, secure her moon pendant through the ancient rites. She had defied him once, had slipped away like smoke through his fingers, but not again. Tonight, she would take her rightful place at his side, would become the vessel for the prophecy's fulfillment.

Then, with Evelyn secured and her pendant in his possession, he would pursue Jesse. Find him standing helplessly before the unopened dolmen, or perhaps already retreating toward the Njaran village. The man would be easy to convince—what use was a pendant that opened nothing? What value did ancient metal hold when it had failed its only test?

Serat closed his eyes, letting the words of the prophecy wash over him, the ancient language flowing through his mind like a river of fire. He had studied these leaves for years, had pored over every line and symbol, searching for the key to unlocking their secrets. And now, with both amulets within his grasp, he knew that his time had finally come.

But there was more to it than that, more than just the fulfillment of an ancient prophecy. For Serat, this was personal, a chance to claim what had always been rightfully his. Evelyn, the woman who had haunted his dreams and consumed his waking thoughts, the woman who had been taken from him so cruelly, so long ago.

He could still remember the day she had disappeared, could still feel the ache of her absence like a physical wound. He had searched for her, had scoured the jungle and the villages, had whispered her name to the spirits and the stars. But she had vanished, as if swallowed by the earth itself, leaving him hollow and broken, a shell of the man he had once been.

But now, with the prophecy on the brink of fulfillment, with the power of both pendants within his grasp, Serat knew that his time had come. He would claim Evelyn as his own, would bind her to him with the ancient rites and rituals of the Oxychana. And together, they would rule, would usher in a new age of power and prosperity for their people.

The Ogham leaves whispered their secrets, their promises, and Serat felt a surge of exultation. The outsider's pendant would come easily—what man would cling to a useless trinket when offered wisdom and belonging? Jesse would hand it over gratefully, eager to be rid of the reminder of his failure.

Serat traced the lines of the final Ogham leaf, feeling the power that thrummed beneath his fingertips. The Heart of the Earth Mother, the source of all life and magic, the key to unlocking the very fabric of reality itself. With both amulets in his command, there would be nothing he could not achieve, no dream that would remain out of reach.

And Evelyn, his beautiful, precious Evelyn, would be by his side, the queen to his king, the mother of his children. Together, they would forge a new world, a world where the Oxychana reigned supreme, where the secrets of the ancients were theirs to wield.

With a final, reverent touch of the leaves, Serat turned and made his way back up the stairs, back to the world above. The torch guttered and danced in his hand, casting flickering shadows on the walls, but he paid them no heed. His mind was already racing ahead, already planning and plotting, weaving the threads of the future into a tapestry of his own design.

The ceremony awaited. Evelyn awaited. And afterward, a simple matter of collecting the second pendant from a defeated man who would be grateful to be rid of his burden.

Serat smiled, a slow, deadly curve of his lips. Soon, very soon, all would be as it was meant to be.

The future was waiting, and Serat was ready to claim it, ready to seize his destiny with both hands and never let go. And may the gods have mercy on anyone who stood in his way.

PUNA

XVIII. THE CEREMONY

The painted spiral on Evelyn's belly was drying to the touch. The strokes of the brush had been intimate, almost arousing. Evelyn had sat motionless as Serat's brush glided across her skin, leaving intricate patterns of red and gold in its wake. Cool, thick strokes, a stark contrast to the heat that simmered at the surface. She'd kept her eyes on her mother until the harsh sound of Serat's voice ordered a serving girl to take the cauldron to the square. Then she saw the scars along the young woman's back and remembered how they had been tempered.

Stay alert, Evelyn told herself, fighting the creeping lethargy that threatened to overtake her senses. Whatever happens, stay alert.

The hut was stifling, the air heavy with the scent of herbs and smoke. Evelyn could feel the sweat beading on her brow, trickling down the curve of her spine. She had been a princess and not known the sting of the whip. Only its sounds. The memory of her exemption brought her focus back, and she turned her head away from the troubling sight. Then her eyes fell on Serat's foot, which was atop the chest beside the wicker chair she lay in. It was wrapped in white and black leather and had a cat jumping up its side.

Her breath caught. Jesse's shoes. The familiar Puma logo, the specific wear pattern on the sole—she would know them anywhere. Her heart began to hammer against her ribs, but she forced her expression to remain neutral. Where is Jesse? What have they done to him?

She didn't dare move, didn't dare disturb the delicate balance of the moment. She knew what was expected of her, knew the role she was meant to play. But seeing Jesse's shoes on Serat's feet sent a chill down her spine that had nothing to do with the evening air. He's here. Jesse came for me. And now...

Her eyes flicked to her two-way radio, clipped casually to Serat's sash like a trophy. The little green light still blinked—battery holding, signal searching. He has my radio…

Mohami's voice cut through the silence, low and melodic, filled with a power that Evelyn could almost taste. "You are ready, my child," she said, her fingers brushing across Evelyn's forehead, tracing the lines of the paint. "The spirits have chosen you, have marked you as their own. Tonight, you will take your place among the Oxychana, will claim your birthright and your destiny."

Evelyn swallowed hard, fighting back the sudden surge of nausea. I have to get out of here. I have to find Jesse before... She thought of the life growing inside her, of the child that she and Jesse had created. What kind of future could she offer her baby if she allowed this to continue?

The ceremony. Once it starts, there will be no escape. No choice.

Serat's eyes drifted to the silver chain around Evelyn's neck, to the moon pendant that rested just above her heart. There was a hunger in his gaze, a raw, desperate longing that made Evelyn's skin crawl. She could feel the power of the amulet, could sense the ancient magic that thrummed within the metal. It was a part of her, a piece of her destiny that she couldn't deny.

But not like this. Not as his prize.

Mohami must have sensed the direction of Serat's thoughts, for she reached out, her fingers hovering just above the pendant, not quite touching, but close enough that Evelyn could feel the heat of her skin. "The amulet," she whispered, her voice a sibilant hiss. "The key to the prophecy, the conduit for the power that will remake the world."

Evelyn's heart thundered in her chest, her mind racing with desperate calculation. She had no choice, no escape. Not yet. She had to play along, had to bide her time and wait for her moment. And so she forced a smile, forced herself to meet Mohami's eyes with a steadiness she didn't feel.

"I am honored," she said, the words feeling thick and clumsy on her tongue. "I am ready to take my place, to serve the Oxychana as I was born to do."

Lie. All of it. But they don't need to know that yet.

Mohami's smile was a flash of white in the dimness, her eyes glinting with satisfaction. "Good," she said, her hand trailing down Evelyn's cheek, fingers brushing against the hammering pulse at her throat. "Very good."

Serat stepped back, admiring his handiwork with a critical eye. The paint glistened on Evelyn's skin, the patterns seeming to writhe and dance in the flickering light. She felt exposed, vulnerable, as if the very essence of her being was laid bare for all to see. But beneath the painted spirals, her mind was working, cataloging every detail, every possible advantage.

Jesse's shoes. The radio. The ceremony at sunset.

When Serat leaves for the cellars, when Mother goes to prepare the square...

That's when I run.

As if reading her thoughts—though she prayed the Oxychana hadn't dulled her mental defenses that much—Serat moved closer, his gaze intense. "I will be your man of the sun," he said softly, his words meant for her ears alone while Mohami busied herself arranging ceremonial items.

Evelyn let the sacred herb rest between her teeth and gums, feeling its bitter juice begin to seep into her bloodstream. But she was ready for it this time, had built walls in her mind, compartments where she could hide her true thoughts. Let him think I'm compliant. Let them both think I've accepted this.

"At sunset," Serat continued, his voice carrying a note of triumph. "When I return from the cellars, we shall unite the people."

She nodded submissively, but her eyes tracked to the doorway where late afternoon light slanted across the threshold. Sunset. How long do I have?

Mohami's voice broke the silence, her tone laced with quiet intensity. "The ceremony will begin at sunset," she said, her eyes never leaving Evelyn's face. "You will be presented to the tribe, will take your rightful place as the bearer of the amulet, the vessel for the power that will change everything."

Evelyn nodded, not trusting herself to speak. Her mind was racing, searching for a way out, for a glimmer of hope in the darkness that threatened to consume her. Jesse came here looking for answers about his father. About me. And instead, he's walked into a trap.

I won't let them use us. I won't let them use our child.

The painted spirals on her belly seemed to pulse with their own rhythm, marking her not as sacred, but as claimed. The thought made her sick, but she held her expression steady, let them see only acceptance where rebellion burned bright.

When the time comes, she promised herself, when the moment is right, I'll be ready.

The sun was already beginning its descent toward the horizon. Soon, Serat would leave for the cellars to retrieve whatever artifacts the ceremony required. Soon, her mother would go to prepare the sacred fire.

And then, Jesse's shoes or not, radio or not, she would run.

XIX. THE DOLMEN

Jesse awoke under the shadows of trees, his head throbbing and his mind foggy. The mark on his face, matching the bench's armrest, was a testament to the length of his slumber, though he had no clear recollection of how long he'd been out. The sky above filtered through the canopy in deep purples and oranges—the last light of sunset fading into dusk.

Sunset. The word felt important somehow, urgent, but he couldn't grasp why.

Disoriented and groggy, Jesse pushed himself to his feet, brushing the dust off his elbows and plucking blades of grass from his matted hair. His sandals, worn thin and incongruous with his fine jogging suit, gave him pause. He knew himself better than to steal, but the juxtaposition of his expensive attire and the dilapidated footwear left him puzzled.

The chemical fog in his head made everything feel distant, dreamlike. Whatever cocktail of medications and substances was still circulating—the lithium, the cough syrup, something else that tasted of bitter herbs and smoke—had left his thoughts scattered like leaves in the wind.

"Damn it," he muttered, a flash of clarity breaking through the haze. Early Alzheimer's... now, he found himself in a foreign land, his memory as tattered as his sandals.

Patting down his sweatshirt, he found no wallet. From against a mound of rock that housed a bench, he started across toward the giant gate. A plaque before the chained-off cavern caught his eye, the brass-studded plate bearing an inscription:

Who but I can know the secrets of the unhewn dolmen?

Who but I can reveal the mysteries of the moon?

Who but I can find the secret resting place of the sun?

Jesse scoffed, mumbling, "Who but I would wake up in the middle of nowhere in a shabby pair of sandals?" A bitter laugh escaped him as he stared up at the ancient stone structure. "Who but I?"

If Dad could see me now... The thought came unbidden, sharp with shame and regret. Standing here like a madman, talking to stones, wearing someone else's shoes. He hoped, wherever his father was, that James Bankole couldn't witness this moment of his son's complete unraveling.

Gazing down at his feet, a flicker of recognition sparked in his mind. Bad memories need good markers. His hand drifted to his pant pocket. Something there. A key.

The events of the previous night began to trickle back into his consciousness. He'd given the man his Pumas and his word, risking reputation for a glimpse inside the ancient dwelling. Yet here he was, mere feet from the entrance, having succumbed to a hallucination. A flight above a massive continent and ultimately, to exhaustion.

Jesse approached the chained gate, the ancient padlock looming before him. As he worked the key into the rusted mechanism, the Dolmen revealed itself, a smooth dome rising high above, its perimeter embraced by a ring of sand and lush jungle growth.

The gate yielded just enough for Jesse to squeeze through sideways, the rusted hinges resisting his efforts. Behind him, the chain clattered to the forest floor, the lock among the fallen links.

Approaching the Dolmen, Jesse marveled at the elephant ears flanking the entrance, their glossy leaves folded back like ancient feather fans. His fingertips grazed the smooth stone, seeking a latch or pressure plate. As he circled the structure, a sudden chill emanated from his chest, as if a block of ice had settled beneath his sweater.

Grasping at the cord around his neck, Jesse pulled the amulet free, the sun emblem ablaze with an intense, cold blue light. He twisted in the sand, desperate to distance himself from the searing sensation. Stumbling back against the Dolmen's face, he expected to meet solid resistance, but instead found himself falling through a thin veil of silky fabric.

For a heartbeat, he thought he'd avoided a brutal landing, but the illusion shattered as he plummeted into the space below, the entrance sealing itself above him in the piercing ultraviolet light of the amulet. The inner side of the dome dropped away and he twisted around to try and catch himself as the cold stone steps grazed by. The first landing met him on his hands and knees, and he rolled down the last few steps to the floor below. He had hit the ground hard, the impact reverberating through his bones before unconsciousness dragged him down into its inky depths again.

The darkness that claimed him was complete, a merciful void that swallowed all the confusion, all the chemical chaos in his bloodstream, all the fragments of memory that refused to coalesce into anything resembling truth. In that blackness, Jesse Bankole ceased to exist, leaving behind only questions carved in stone and the echo of ancient words:

Who but I?

XX. THE PURSUIT

The painted spiral on her belly had barely dried when Evelyn made her move. As Serat disappeared down the steps toward the cellars, his stolen shoes—Jesse's shoes—carrying him away from the hut, she rose from the purple pillows like a coiled spring finally released.

Her mother's cries chased her into the gathering dusk—"Do not defy us again, Evelyn! Come back!"—but she was already running, her bare feet flying over the packed earth between the flickering tiki torches.

The wad of quid she spat into the dirt as she fled was more than medicine expelled—it was renunciation, a severing of ties, a final rejection of everything they wanted her to become. She would not be Serat's prize. She would not be anyone's vessel for ancient prophecies.

Jesse is out there. Somewhere. And I will find him.

The jungle pressed in around her as night descended, the canopy above swallowing the last purple light of sunset. Thunder grumbled ominously, the sky itself seeming to mirror her own mounting dread. She'd had a head start, but not much of one.

The first horn blast cleaved the air behind her like a battle cry, the sound making her stumble. Serat had discovered her absence sooner than expected. She could almost see him in her mind's eye—his face contorted in rage as he sounded the alarm, rousing his followers to give chase.

Gritting her teeth, she pushed herself harder, clinging to the hope that she could reach the trading path, maybe even make it to the Njaran village before they caught her.

But then a second horn blast shattered that hope—not from behind her, but from somewhere ahead. Close. Too close.

An answering bellow rose from the village, a brutal call-and-response that sent icy tendrils of fear down her spine. They had anticipated her route, positioned hunters along the path. Despair crashed over her as she crumpled onto a stone bench, her bundle of clothing tumbling from nerveless fingers.

The rain began then, fat drops that quickly became a deluge, soaking through her thin garments and chilling her to the bone. She fumbled for her cell phone, wincing at the bright light of the screen. No service. She wrapped it back with her passport, protecting what little she had left of the outside world.

Then, through the curtain of rain, her eyes caught something that made her heart leap: a flicker of movement across the path, a shimmer that seemed to waver and shift. The dolmen. Its illusion had been broken, the once-veiled entrance revealing itself like a beacon in the storm.

And there—the chain coiled at the base of the gate, left ajar. Among the links, an ancient padlock lay open.

Someone's been here. Recently.

Hope kindled in her chest like a flame in the darkness. She thought of the old stories, the legends her mother had told her as a child about the sacred site that could shelter those in desperate need.

Maybe it's not too late.

Thunder crashed overhead as she gathered her belongings and ran toward the gate, toward whatever sanctuary the ancient stones might offer. Behind her, the hunting horns grew closer, but ahead lay possibility—and perhaps, if the fates were kind, the man she'd come so far to save.

XXI. THE LIGHT

Father Time leans back in his worn La-Z-Boy, his bowl of popcorn sloshing into his lap. He fiddles with the magiscope's remote and gets the crystal sphere between the golden dragons going again. Mother Earth climbs into his chair with him, snuggling against him, and again spilling his popcorn. He flicks off a few kernels and scowls.

"Ooh, this is it!" she squeals, pointing at the swirling vision in the sphere. "This is the best part, honey!"

"Yeah, yeah," Father Time mutters, but he's grinning as he wraps his arm around her. "Just don't spoil it for me. I know that memory of yours."

Inside the magiscope, the image sharpened to reveal a man sprawled on cold stone, ethereal blue light dancing around his prone form like living aurora.

The man looked up from his back through the intruding darkness, the outside world giving way to an ethereal azure glow that seemed to suffuse the very air around him. A light persisted—a radiant point of brilliance that pierced the veil of oblivion, drawing him back to the surface.

"Oh, look at him," Mother Earth coos, pressing closer to her husband. "Poor baby doesn't know where he is."

"Hey, dramatic tension," Father Time shrugs, taking great pains to reach his mouth for another gulp of beer.

The vision in the crystal sphere swirled, showing Jesse's confused face as he struggled to focus, his thoughts scattered like debris in a hurricane.

The man's head throbbed with a crushing weight, thoughts dancing like leaves in a storm. The fall, the drugs still coursing through his system, the chemical fog that made everything feel distant and strange—it all pressed down on him like a weight he couldn't lift.

A voice drifted through the haze, desperate and beautiful, tugging at something deep inside him that he couldn't quite reach. The sun pendant blazed with uncanny blue light, pulsing with otherworldly energy.

"There she is!" Mother Earth bounces excitedly. "Our girl! Look at those pendants go—sun and moon, baby!"

Father Time nearly chokes. "Cool your jets!" he says. "Hell of a light show though."

"I know, right?" Mother Earth fans herself with the cosmic TV Guide. "I think it's hot. But you know that it gets me every time."

Within the magiscope, Evelyn appeared at the threshold like an angel of mercy, her moon pendant blazing crimson as she descended the ancient steps.

Evelyn stood at the opening of the dolmen, her heart hammering as she took in the impossible sight. The entrance's disguise lay in tatters, revealing the yawning mouth of ancient stone. As she grasped the torn fabric, her moon pendant flared to life, crimson light spilling down the stone steps.

"Jesse?!" Her voice echoed in the cavernous space.

"Oh no," Mother Earth gasps, clutching Father Time's arm. "He doesn't recognize her!"

"Relax, babe," Father Time pats her hand. "Trust the process."

The image in the crystal sphere showed Jesse's vacant stare, his beautiful blue eyes empty of recognition as Evelyn went to kneel beside him in growing desperation.

The man below stirred, struggling to focus, but his eyes stared at her with blank incomprehension. The concussion, the chemicals, the trauma—it had stolen him from her just when she needed him most.

She knelt beside him, searching those vacant eyes for recognition. "It's me," she whispered. "It's Evelyn. Please, Jesse, you have to remember."

The hunting horns echoed from above—closer, much closer.

"Get up, Jesse!" she cried. "Get up! They're coming!"

"Oh, this is killing me," Mother Earth whimpers. "How can she save them both if he doesn't even know who she is?"

"Wait for it..." Father Time grins wickedly.

But he only stared, confusion clouding his features. The pendant pulsed at her throat. Rising on her toes, she pressed her lips to his, pouring all her love into that desperate kiss.

For a heartbeat, nothing. Then something shifted behind his eyes—a spark, like dawn breaking.

"Evelyn," he breathed. "My Evelyn."

"YESSS!" Mother Earth pumps her fist in the air, spilling popcorn everywhere. "That's my girl! True love's kiss for the win!"

Father Time made a breathy laugh. "Look at that—boom! Memory restored. Classic." He scoffed.

Mother Earth almost gave him a playful slap but saw he was actually fighting back tears. "You're such a romantic," Mother Earth sighs, nuzzling against his neck. "You, see? It gets us both."

The crystal sphere pulsed with warm light as it showed the lovers again.

Relief flooded through her as his arms came around her, solid and real.

"They're coming," she whispered. "Serat betrayed you. We have to run."

Understanding flashed in his eyes. He was Jesse again, her protector.

"Where?" he asked.

Father Time's grip tightens on Mother Earth as they watch the scene unfold. "And here we go, baby. The grand finale."

Mother Earth shivers with anticipation. "Ooh, what they're about to find down there... it's going to blow their minds. I'm always impressed with your work."

Within the magiscope, the image shifted to show the tunnel entrance.

Evelyn gestured toward the tunnel where quartz veins caught their pendants' light and threw it back in cascading rivers of fire.

"There," she said. "Into the heart of it all."

Father Time grins, pulling his wife closer as the crystal sphere pulses with anticipation. "I can't take all the credit," he says, planting a kiss on her temple.

The vision in the magiscope followed the two lovers as they joined hands and stepped into the luminous tunnel, their combined light painting ancient prophecies on walls that had waited millennia to be fulfilled.

XXII. THE CHAMBER

The cloak of Paeden.... Serat had thought it a myth. Now it was draped around him, taken from the entrance. Activated by the proximity of the brooches. Only the light of his torch was visible now as he moved along the dark corridor of the dolmen. Perhaps the legends of King Arthur were true. Perhaps the device at the heart of their Tribe's most sacred site was also real? Whether or not he caught the fleeing couple before they activated the device, he would find out how far the truth of the leaf totem houses went.

"They know not what they do," he murmured, as he padded along swiftly under the cloak of invisibility and silently in his new footwear.

~

Evelyn and I raced through the twisting passages, but as we ran, something extraordinary began to happen. The light from our amulets didn't simply illuminate the path ahead—it was being drawn away from us, pulled into the walls themselves like water finding its course.

I looked up to see twin veins of quartz running along either side of the tunnel, one drinking in Evelyn's crimson radiance, the other absorbing my pendant's ethereal blue. The light didn't just seep into the stone—it raced ahead of us like liquid fire, two bright sparks speeding down perfectly straight crystalline channels into the darkness beyond.

"We have to keep up with it," I panted, pushing myself harder as the sparks shot forward with relentless speed. The tunnel stretched endlessly ahead, the quartz veins running true as arrows, our only illumination those twin points of racing light that seemed determined to outpace us.

We ran and ran, our footsteps echoing in the darkness behind the fleeing radiance. My lungs burned, and beside me, Evelyn's breathing came in sharp gasps, but still we pressed on, chasing those elusive sparks through what felt like miles of ancient stone.

Then, gradually, something changed. The sparks began to slow, the arrow-straight veins starting to curve and spiral. I felt a moment's relief as we finally began to close the distance, but the memory of the hunting horns still echoed behind us, spurring my urgency.

"We need to keep moving," I urged, glancing nervously over my shoulder as the sparks sizzled and danced along the curving veins like twin fuses. "If they're coming, they'll be close."

But now we had no choice but to wait. The tunnel ahead was plunged into absolute darkness until the lights completed their artistic work, each spark following its meandering path with painstaking precision.

To Evelyn's right, circles and spirals bloomed into delicate seashells, into intricate conchs and shimmering mother-of-pearl. Clams and shrimp, crabs and lobsters, all rendered in exquisite detail, seemed to flutter and dance in the lambent glow.

On my left, seedlings unfurled into lush foliage, vines twining and flowers blooming in a riot of ultraviolet blue. Bees and butterflies, rendered in light, flitted among the petals, while caterpillars inched along the leaves, spinning gossamer threads that glittered like diamonds.

"Evelyn, look!" I gasped, my eyes wide with wonder. "It's like the whole history of life on Earth, playing out before our eyes."

She nodded, her gaze darting from one marvel to the next, transfixed despite the danger behind us. "It's incredible. It's like the tunnel is alive, like it's responding to the power of the amulets." Her voice carried that same wonder I remembered from when she'd painted Notre-Dame from our Paris window. "This reminds me of the creation stories my mother told me—when all life emerged from the Earth Mother's embrace."

As we pressed onward, the creatures on the walls grew larger, more complex. Fish and amphibians gave way to reptiles and birds, each one picked out in painstaking detail, each scale and feather limned in light. Mammals emerged from the shadows—rodents and bats, jungle cats and primates, all caught in frozen tableaus of predator and prey, of nurture and instinct.

And then, in a staggering feat of artistry, the images began to move, to flow together like a living tapestry. On one side, animals submitting to the yoke of domestication, learning to live and work alongside their human masters. On the other, the primal dance of procreation, of mothers heavy with child, of infants taking their first tentative steps.

I felt tears prick at the corners of my eyes, overwhelmed by the sheer beauty of it, by the staggering scope of the vision playing out before us. My protective urgency warred with growing awe as even I couldn't help but be moved by what we were witnessing. I reached for Evelyn's hand, lacing my fingers through hers, feeling the pulse of the amulets' power thrumming between our joined palms.

And then, as the tunnel widened into a vaulted cavern, the images changed once more. Countless figures, all picked out in glowing lines of red and blue, marched in lockstep up the sides of a towering pyramid, each one bearing a golden block upon their shoulders. The walls of the chamber itself seemed to be composed of the same precious metal, gleaming with an inner fire that kindled the senses and quickened the blood.

At the far end of the cavern, the two halves of the mural converged, the figures uniting in a single, harmonious purpose. A great eye, radiant with an otherworldly white light, blazed from the capstone of the pyramid, bathing the chamber in its luminous gaze. And there, at the center of it all, a door began to appear, etched in lines of searing brilliance.

"The entrance to the inner sanctum," Evelyn breathed.

I stepped forward, my hand outstretched, my fingers brushing against the glowing lines. At my touch, the door swung open, soundless and weightless, revealing a chamber beyond.

We stood on the threshold for a breathless moment, drinking in the sight. The room was smaller than the cavern that housed it, but no less majestic, its every surface polished to a mirror sheen. The floor reflected our awed expressions back at us, twin portraits of wonder and trepidation.

As we stepped inside, the light from the outer chamber dimmed, fading away as if drawn upward into the vaulted recesses of the ceiling. In its place, a soft, silver radiance began to emanate from above, casting the room in a dreamlike glow.

Evelyn turned in a slow circle, her eyes widening as she took in the walls around us. To our right, a towering wave of gold and jewels crested and broke against a lone figure, a man clad all in silver, his shield raised in defiant resistance against the onslaught of riches.

On the left, another figure, this one robed in gold, stood with arm upraised, a flaming sword clasped in his fist. Before him, a swirling vortex of silver seemed to bend to his will, drawn into a shimmering column of power that stretched toward the ceiling above.

"The eternal struggle between earthly wealth and divine purpose," I murmured, my voice echoing strangely in the stillness. "The choice that faces every one of us, in the end."

Evelyn started to reply, but a sound from behind cut her short, a soft footfall that sent a chill skittering down my spine. We spun around, hearts in our throats, just as a crack of thunder boomed overhead.

A jagged bolt of lightning split the silver canopy above, spidering out in a dizzying web of crackling energy. The air sizzled and hummed, alive with the raw force of the tempest, and for a moment, the chamber was plunged into darkness.

But as our eyes adjusted to the gloom, a new light began to bloom at the far end of the room, a radiant emerald glow that limned the contours of a towering tree. Its branches stretched toward the ceiling, each one studded with gleaming green gems that winked and glittered like fallen stars.

At the base of the tree, two figures sat, their forms intertwined in an embrace that seemed to defy the bounds of mere stone. Man and woman, their limbs entangled, their faces lifted to the heavens, they held out their cupped hands in a gesture of offering and supplication.

As Evelyn and I drew closer, we saw that the statues' eyes were no lifeless orbs of carved quartz, but living, shining pools of darkness. They stared down at the mirrored floor, at the reflected glory of the chamber around them, and for a moment, it seemed as though the whole world had been inverted, turned upside down and inside out.

"Look," Evelyn gasped, pointing to the figures' outstretched hands. "The amulet!"

And there, cradled in the stone palms, a shimmering vortex of color had begun to swirl, a kaleidoscope of hues that pulsed in time with heartbeat. At their centers, an image began to coalesce, a perfect, miniature rendering of the Earth in all her glory.

Evelyn fumbled with her amulet, holding it out to the light. It flared in her grasp, a riot of iridescent color that danced and spun in perfect synchronicity with the vortex in the statue's hand.

I reached for her, my fingers closing over her own, the metal warm and thrumming with power between our joined palms. For a moment we stood transfixed, caught in the grip of something vast and ancient, something that reached out from the very heart of creation to touch our souls.

And then, like a thunderclap, a voice boomed out, shaking the chamber to its very foundations.

"Eve! The relic, now!"

But it wasn't the voice of any god or spirit. The echoes died away and as the ringing in our ears began to fade, my gaze fell to the mirrored floor at our feet. And there, in the polished surface, was the reflection of my old pumas.

XXIII. THE END OF THE BEGINNING

With a single, swift motion, Serat cast the cloak from around his shoulders, his form rolling into view. The fabric shimmered as it twisted through the air. In the same heartbeat, he seized Evelyn, one powerful arm wrapping around her throat, pulling her tight against his chest.

Evelyn gasped, the amulet slipping from her grasp to clatter against the mirrored floor. Her fingers scrabbled at Serat's forearm, desperate to break his hold, but his grip was iron, unyielding.

I lunged for them, my heart in my throat, my blood pounding in my ears. But even as I reached for Evelyn, Serat's other hand flashed out, and the wicked curve of a blade gleamed in the chamber's eerie light. The scimitar, that cruel, curved knife, hovered a hairsbreadth from Evelyn's throat, the threat clear in every line of Serat's body.

Rage and desperation warred within me, a red haze descending over my vision. I could see the madness in Serat's eyes, the twisted triumph that bordered on obsession. This was a man pushed to the brink, a man who had sacrificed everything for the promise of power, for the chance to claim what he believed was rightfully his.

My hand closed around Serat's wrist, my fingers digging into the corded muscle, trying to wrench the blade away from Evelyn's vulnerable flesh. But Serat was far stronger than I had anticipated. Even with both hands straining against him, I could feel my grip beginning to slip, my strength failing in the face of his manic determination.

I sank to one knee, the mirrored floor cold and unyielding beneath me. Sweat beaded on my brow, my teeth clenched as I fought to hold back the killing blow. But it was a losing battle, and we both knew it.

Just as I thought my arms would give out, just as I braced myself for the bite of the blade, Serat let out a howl of pain. His grip on Evelyn loosened, and she tumbled to the floor, sliding across the smooth surface to fetch up against the far wall. In the same instant, a crack of thunder split the air, and a bolt of silver lightning seared through the heart of the emerald tree, setting the chamber ablaze with light.

I saw Evelyn crouched against the wall, one hand pressed to her mouth, a smear of blood staining her chin. She had bitten Serat, had used the only weapon at her disposal to buy us a precious few seconds of reprieve.

But Serat was already recovering, his eyes flashing with murderous intent. He lunged for the amulet where it lay, his fingers brushing against the iridescent surface. "You know nothing of such power," he snarled, his voice ragged with pain and fury.

Desperation gave me strength, and I surged to my feet, a wordless cry tearing from my throat. I slammed into Serat with all the force I could muster, my shoulder driving into his ribs with a sickening crack. We went down in a tangle of limbs, the scimitar skittering across the floor, out of reach.

But Serat was far from defeated. With a twist of his body, he rolled, pinning me beneath him. His elbow dug into my windpipe, his weight bearing down on me like a crushing vise. Stars burst behind my eyes, the edges of my vision going dark as I clawed at his arm, at his face, desperate for air.

The blow, when it came, exploded against my jaw, snapping my head to the side. I tasted blood, felt the white-hot flare of pain as Serat drew back his fist for another strike. But before he could land the blow, Evelyn was there, her arms wrapping around his throat from behind, wrenching him away from me.

Serat roared, his hand tangling in Evelyn's hair, yanking her off balance. They fell together, a writhing mass of fury, and I saw Serat's fingers close around the hilt of the fallen scimitar.

Evelyn's eyes met mine, wide with fear and determination. In that suspended moment, I saw the resolve in her gaze, the unwavering strength that had carried her this far. She knew, as I did, that we were fighting not just for our own lives, but for something far greater, something that reached beyond the boundaries of flesh and bone.

I rolled to my knees, every breath a struggle, my lungs burning with the need for air. Serat towered over us, the scimitar poised to strike, his face a mask of rage and madness.

"It's an abomination!" he spat, his eyes burning with a fevered light. "You're siblings!"

The words hit the chamber like a thunderclap. I felt my blood turn to ice, but as I looked at Evelyn, I saw something unexpected in her eyes—not shock, but a terrible, knowing sadness. She already knew. Had known.

Serat's face contorted with triumph as he watched for our devastation. "Brother and sister!" he snarled. "The blood of James flows through you both!"

But instead of the horror he expected, Evelyn and I locked eyes. In that moment, I understood that she had been carrying this knowledge, this burden. And she could see in my face that I had suspected, had feared this very truth.

"We know," I said quietly, never breaking eye contact with Evelyn. "And we're still here."

Serat's expression faltered, confusion replacing his savage glee. He had thrown his greatest weapon, and it had failed to destroy us.

That moment of uncertainty was all I needed. I lunged forward again, lifting his hand that held the scimitar. But as I struggled to break his grip, his other hand tore my amulet away and it went sliding across the chamber floor toward the door.

He wrenched his sword hand free, sending me careening by, and his eyes followed the sliding relic to where it stopped at someone's feet. Everything went suddenly silent and still. And I turned to look up from where I'd fallen.

"Jesse!" The voice cut through the tumult like a blade, sharp and commanding. My heart hammered against my ribs when I saw Greg standing beside the open door, the sun amulet clutched in his outstretched hand.

Serat stood, staring at Greg, motionless with caution and confusion.

"Your father's debt," Greg said, his eyes meeting mine with profound gravity. "I promised James I'd see this through. The girls are safe in Athens—this was always about protecting his children."

Serat eyes were wide with shock and fury. He took a stumbling step forward, the scimitar raised in a gesture of defiance. But Greg held his ground, his gaze steady, the amulet pulsing with strange tendrils of light reaching toward the male statue's upturned palm.

What happened next was a blur of motion, an act of desperation. Serat lunged, the scimitar flashing in a deadly arc. The blade sank deep into Greg's flesh, and I heard Evelyn's scream, saw the spray of crimson that painted Serat's face. The amulet fell, skating across the floor toward us.

Greg pulled Serat close, his fingers locked around the blade's hilt, a final, defiant act of courage.

I surged forward, the need to reach them, to save Greg, consuming every thought. But Evelyn's hand closed around my arm, her grip fierce and unyielding.

"Jesse, the door!" Greg gasped.

I turned, understanding dawning. The great golden door was swinging shut, the light of the chamber dimming as the opening narrowed. Greg was drawing Serat back through the entrance. I threw my back against the door and it slid like a puck on ice. Through the gap, torchlight of a dozen villagers approaching was cut off as the door closed with a resounding boom.

The sound echoed through the chamber like the tolling of a funeral bell. For a moment, all was stillness and silence, the only movement the lazy shifting prisms of light in the chamber above.

I knelt beside Evelyn, my hands finding hers in the fading light. Her eyes were wide and haunted, tears tracing glistening paths down her cheeks.

"Greg," she whispered, the word a broken plea.

"He saved us," I murmured, the truth of it settling like a weight in my chest.

"He's out there!" she said, her voice rising with panic.

I shook my head, running my hand along the seam where white light was just now disappearing. "There isn't..." The door was gone. The chamber was now a floor of mirrors, silver and grey clouds above and below, ball lightning tumbling through the metallic surfaces of the ceiling and glistening in eruptions of emerald green from the leaves.

She nodded, her jaw clenched with resolve. But as she turned to face me, I saw a new uncertainty flicker in her gaze—not about our blood, but about what came next.

"Jesse," she said softly, her voice barely above a whisper. "When he said siblings... you didn't seem surprised."

I swallowed hard, the words sticking in my throat. "I found things in my father's journals. Maps, a picture of your mother. " I met her eyes. "I suspected we might be... half-siblings."

"Not half," Evelyn said quietly, her hand moving to cover mine. "Your father came to my mother twice. Once when you were conceived, and again a year later." Her voice grew softer. "We're full brother and sister, Jesse."

The weight of the complete truth settled between us. I searched her face, seeing the fear there—not of what we were, but of how I would react.

"You've known," I said. It wasn't a question.

"Since I returned to the village. My mother told me about the son who came before me." Tears spilled down her cheeks. "I was terrified you would hate me for not telling you. For letting us..."

I pulled her close, my arms encircling her as the chamber continued its mystical transformation around us. "We didn't know," I whispered fiercely. "We loved each other in innocence, Evelyn. That love isn't tainted by knowledge that came after."

"But Greg," she said against my shoulder, her voice breaking with grief and panic. "He didn't have to die for us! We could have found another way!"

"Why did he do that?" I pulled back, frantic, my hands shaking. "He threw his life away! There had to be another option!"

Evelyn reached for my hands, trying to calm me. "Jesse, he promised your father. He told me on the way here that he owed a debt to James, that he'd made a promise to see this through..."

I stopped, my mind racing back to my father's papers. "A debt..." The memory surfaced slowly. "There was something in father's notes. 'Research partner still owes outstanding debt. Will honor agreement when needed.'" I looked at her with dawning understanding. "Greg was... he was father's colleague. This whole time, he was watching over us because of a promise."

Evelyn nodded, tears in her eyes. "He knew what we were to each other, Jesse. He knew, and he still protected us. He said it was his responsibility to see it through to the end."

Around us, the chamber began to shift and change, the light from the emerald tree spilling across the walls in a dazzling display. The statues' eyes blazed with renewed vigor, their hands cupping kaleidoscopes of color that swirled with images of the Earth itself.

The truth hung in the air between us, heavy and inescapable. I reached for her, my hands cradling her face, my thumbs brushing away the tears that spilled anew. "Evelyn," I whispered, my voice rough with emotion. "Whatever the truth of our blood, of our parentage, it doesn't change what we are to each other. It doesn't change what I feel for you."

She leaned into my touch, her eyes fluttering closed. "There's more, Jesse," she said softly, her hand coming to rest on the gentle swell of her belly. "The child I carry, the life we created together..."

My heart clenched, a fierce, protective warmth spreading through my veins. I drew her close, my lips brushing against her temple, my arms holding her as if I could shield her from all the pain and uncertainty of the world.

"And there is no doubt?" I paused. I thought of the girls. Of Greg. "That it is…"

"Jesse," she said. "I was always faithful to you. I knew before you left."

Silence stretched. Eventually, I caressed her now obvious round abdomen. "Our child," I murmured, wonder and awe mingling with the love that burned bright within me. "Born of an ancient legacy."

Evelyn and I rose to our feet, our hands clasped, our hearts beating as one. We turned to face the shimmering vortexes that swirled within the stone palms, images of the Earth itself, born anew in a crucible of light and shadow.

"There was a time," I said softly, the words a benediction, a vow, "when all of humanity was of one blood, one soul. What we have found here, Evelyn, what we have discovered within ourselves...it is a reminder of that fundamental truth. A truth that transcends the boundaries of tribe and tradition, of history and circumstance."

She nodded, her eyes shining with a fierce, unwavering love. "In the beginning," she murmured, echoing the tales of her own people, "the Earth Mother poured her essence into all living things, binding us together in a web of creation. What we have done, Jesse, in coming together, in forging a bond that defies the dictates of the past...it is an affirmation of that primal connection, that fundamental unity."

I drew her to me, my lips finding hers in a kiss that seared my soul, that burned away the last vestiges of doubt and fear. In that moment, as the chamber shuddered with the force of a power older than time itself, I knew that we had found our destiny, our purpose.

The amulets flared with blinding radiance, the light engulfing us. I picked up the sun pendant, its spider-fine tendrils of light reaching toward the swirling miasma in the male statue's hand. Evelyn's amulet reached out in holographic form toward the female likeness of stone. Both hands had rainbows of circling light, ebbing and flowing, rising and falling like crowns centered on each palm.

"What must we do?" I asked, my voice steady despite the tremor of awe that rippled through me.

I felt the weight of the amulet in my hand, the pulse of its power a living thing, a promise of some changed future that awaited us. Beside me, Evelyn stood tall and proud, her eyes alight with the fire of her moon amulet and of her own unshakable conviction.

We both gazed at the kaleidoscope of colors swirling in the stone palms—perfect renditions of our pendants, waiting, calling to us. The chamber thrummed with ancient power, the very air crackling with possibility.

Evelyn and I looked at each other, understanding passing between us without words. Whatever lay ahead, whatever cosmic forces we were about to unleash, we had made our choice long ago in a London inn, reaffirmed it in Paris, and sealed it here in the heart of the earth itself.

"Together," she said, her voice ringing with the clarity of a bell.

I nodded, my heart swelling with courage and love. "Together," I echoed.

XXIV. EGYPT

Abbott Bruner's fascination with Egypt, particularly the Great Pyramid and the Sphinx, had consumed him for countless years. As an Egyptologist, he relished any opportunity to share his knowledge, often leading amateur expeditions that showcased his infectious enthusiasm. His wife, Anna, had journeyed from their home in Southern Seoul to join him on this latest venture, a cherished tradition they shared.

As the group approached the Giza site on camelback, Abbott Bruner began his well-practiced dialogue, his voice carrying over the gentle sway of the beasts beneath them. "The Great Pyramid is a marvel of engineering," he explained, gesturing to the towering structure that loomed ahead. "The sheer weight of the stone required a foundation of immense strength and stability. Beneath the shifting sands, a solid granite mountain provides that base, though the depths to which the pyramid extends remain a mystery."

Jarred, a senior paleontology student from UGA, raised a questioning eyebrow in the days lingering warmth. "Hasn't anyone explored the site, Abbott? Surely someone must know what lies beneath."

Abbott Bruner smiled, the pyramid's majestic form dwarfing the surrounding adobe buildings, their rectangular lines softened by the ravages of time. "Archaeologists have been fortunate indeed that Egypt has allowed any expeditions at all," he replied, his tone measured. "It's a delicate subject, fraught with political and cultural sensitivities. But sometimes, it's in the contemplation of such mysteries that we find the greatest discoveries - not of fact, but of imagination."

"But what about the ground-penetrating radar discoveries?" Jarred pressed, his voice rising with excitement. "The massive shaft systems they've found extending for miles beneath the pyramid - connecting to networks under Europe, Africa, even the Americas?"

Abbott Bruner's smile became slightly strained. "Ah, someone's been watching too much YouTube, I see."

"It's not YouTube!" Jarred protested, his academic pride stung. "These are peer-reviewed studies! The radar shows tunnel networks that could span continents!"

Anna hid a smile behind her hand, watching her husband's diplomatic composure being tested by an enthusiastic student armed with internet research.

"Perhaps," Abbott said carefully, "we should focus on what we can observe with our own eyes rather than chase theories that..." He trailed off, glancing at Anna's amused expression. "Well, let's just say that extraordinary claims require extraordinary evidence."

Abbott Bruner's eyes sparkled with mischief as he addressed the group once more, eager to change the subject. "Does anyone happen to have an American dollar bill on hand?"

The woman in the beige safari outfit, her sandy blonde hair twisted into a neat bun beneath her wide-brimmed hat, rummaged in her vest pocket and produced a crumpled note. Abbott Bruner accepted it with a grateful nod, smoothing the bill against the worn leather of his saddle.

"Take a look here," he said, holding the dollar up against the backdrop of the pyramid. "The illustration on the right, with the capstone separated from the base and the all-seeing eye of Ra at its center. Some say it represents the notion that only a fraction of the pyramid's true form is visible to us today. The rest, they claim, is buried deep within the earth itself, a mystery waiting to be unraveled."

As they drew closer to the monument, the velvet ropes of the tourist queue coming into view, Abbott Bruner continued his lecture, his voice rising with excitement. "The precision of the pyramid's construction is staggering. It faces true north with an accuracy that defies belief - the odds of such perfect alignment are less than one in three billion. And its location, situated at the exact center of the Earth's landmass, at zero degrees latitude and longitude? It's a feat of engineering and geography that boggles the mind."

The group dismounted, tethering their camels to the wooden posts that lined the bustling marketplace. Hawkers were packing away their displayed miniature figurines and replica mummies, their voices rising in a cacophony of enticement. Abbott Bruner helped Anna down from her mount, his touch gentle as he adjusted her bonnet and pressed a kiss to her cheek.

"Will the wonder of this place ever fade, my love?" he murmured, his eyes alight with boyish glee.

Jason, a student from Harvard, approached the couple, his brow furrowed in thought. "Abbott, you mentioned the blocks used in the pyramid's construction. Were they quarried from nearby?"

Abbott Bruner nodded, his expression grave. "Some were indeed brought from distant quarries, many weighing several tons apiece. But the pyramid we see today is a mere shadow of its former glory. In its original state, it would have been even more breathtaking."

"How so?" Jason asked, leaning forward in rapt attention.

"When the Great Pyramid was first completed," Abbott Bruner explained, "it was encased in blocks of polished white limestone, cut and fitted with exquisite precision. They would have gleamed in the sun like mirrors, reflecting the light in a dazzling display. What remains now is the underlying core, the skeleton of the once-resplendent whole."

Anna tilted her head back, her gaze tracing the lines of the pyramid until it reached the peak, where the capstone thrust into the late afternoon desert sky. Around her, the others peppered Abbott Bruner with questions, their curiosity insatiable.

"What lies within these pyramids, Abbott?" one asked, her voice hushed with awe.

Abbott Bruner's eyes glittered in the low western sun, his tone conspiratorial. "Most were built as burial chambers for the great pharaohs, their treasures meant to accompany them into the afterlife. But more often than not, those riches were plundered long before modern archaeologists ever set foot inside. The true challenge, however, lies in the depths of the pyramids themselves. The winding passageways and hidden chambers are so far removed from the surface that oxygen is scarce, and torches sputter and die in the thin air. Only with the advent of electric light have we been able to pierce those final veils of darkness and explore the furthest reaches of these ancient tombs."

"But how did the builders manage it, then?" the young woman pressed, her brow furrowed in confusion. "If even torches won't burn that deep, how did they create such intricate and beautiful spaces?"

Abbott Bruner's smile was enigmatic, his eyes alight with the thrill of the unknown. "Ah, now that's a question that has puzzled scholars and scientists for generations. One theory suggests that the network of ventilation shafts was designed to provide both air and light, but many of those passages have long since collapsed or shifted, making it impossible to say for certain."

He glanced at Anna, seeing the warning in her eyes, the gentle admonishment not to stray too far into the realm of the fantastical. But the spark of passion was kindling in his chest, the irresistible lure of the unknown, and he couldn't help but fan the flames.

"There are other theories, of course," he said, lowering his voice as if imparting a great secret. "Stranger, more wondrous explanations that challenge the very foundations of our understanding. The world is full of such mysteries - perfectly machined artifacts buried in ancient coal seams, dinosaur bones bearing the marks of bullets, things that shouldn't be possible and yet...there they are."

The blonde woman's eyes were wide, her voice breathless with excitement. "Bullets in dinosaur bones? But that's...that's impossible!"

Abbott Bruner's grin was infectious, his enthusiasm bubbling over like a wellspring. "And yet, it's true! Just as true as the ancient batteries found in Egyptian tombs, devices that predate the invention of the modern battery by thousands of years. Crafted from simple materials like fruit acids and copper, they hint at a level of technological sophistication that defies our understanding of the past."

The young woman shook her head, wonder and disbelief warring in her eyes. "But Giza...the pyramids...they're ancient! How could they have had such knowledge, such capabilities, so long ago?"

Abbott Bruner's laughter was gentle, his tone indulgent. "Oh, my dear, you have no idea just how ancient this place truly is. The most conservative estimates place the construction of the Giza complex around 2500 BCE. But there are those who believe it to be far, far older - ten thousand years, perhaps even fifteen. The secrets buried beneath these sands could rewrite the very history of human civilization as we know it."

Anna cleared her throat, a gentle reminder for her husband to rein in his more fanciful speculations. "Perhaps we should focus on the wonders that surround us, dear," she murmured, her hand resting on his arm. "This is an evening trip, and there is only so much sunlight available. "

Abbott Bruner's smile was rueful, his nod acknowledging the wisdom of her words. "Of course, of course. Forgive an old man's flights of fancy." He turned to the group, his arm sweeping out to encompass the distant figure of the Sphinx, its leonine body crouched in eternal vigil. "Take the Sphinx, for example. Did you know that its gaze is said to be aligned with the star system of Sirius, the brightest in the night sky? In ancient texts, Sirius is often described as the home of the gods, the place from which divine knowledge and power flows to earth."

Andy, one of the younger students, stepped forward, his eyes alight with curiosity. "And the pyramid itself, Abbott? You said it represents something - an hourglass, a symbol of endings and beginnings?"

Abbott Bruner nodded, his expression grave. "Indeed, my boy. The Great Pyramid, with its distinctive shape and its alignment with the celestial bodies, has long been associated with the concept of cyclical time, of the great wheel of existence. Some believe that when certain cosmic alignments occur - the convergence of Sirius with the black hole at its heart, for example - a new age will dawn, a time of transformation and rebirth."

Andy's eyes widened, his voice trembling with a mixture of excitement and trepidation. "And when is this alignment supposed to happen, Abbott?"

Abbott Bruner's smile was cryptic, his eyes sparkling with mirth. "Why do you think I was so insistent on being here today, of all days?"

Andy's jaw dropped, his face a mask of shocked realization. "You mean...it's today? The alignment is happening now?"

Abbott Bruner's laughter rang out, rich and deep, as he clapped the young man on the shoulder. "Relax, my boy. Relax. While it's true that some have posited a link between the Great Pyramid and the biblical Tower of Babel, a structure meant to unite humanity in a single, glorious purpose, I think we can safely say that the secrets of the ancients will keep a little while longer."

But even as the words left his lips, a strange stillness descended over the plateau, a hush that seemed to swallow all sound. Christi, still struggling with her camel's tether, cried out in alarm as the beast suddenly reared, its eyes rolling in terror. All around them, the other animals began to stamp and snort, their agitation palpable in the heat.

Abbott Bruner's gaze snapped to the pyramid, his heart stuttering in his chest as a plume of sand billowed from the capstone, a shimmering veil that caught the remaining light like a shroud of gold. Rivulets of sand began to cascade down the weathered blocks, a waterfall of glistening grains that pooled at the base and began to churn, as if stirred by an unseen hand.

The sound was like nothing any of them had ever heard before, a deep, grinding rumble that seemed to emanate from the very bones of the earth. It rose in pitch and intensity, a roar that drowned out the cries of the camels as they wrenched free of their tethers and bolted into the desert, their hooves churning up great clouds of dust in their wake.

"My God," Abbott Bruner breathed, his voice barely audible over the growing cacophony. "It can't be..."

But even as the words left his lips, the truth of what he was seeing crashed over him like a wave, stealing the breath from his lungs and sending a bolt of pure, unadulterated awe shivering down his spine. For it wasn't the sand that was moving, wasn't the earth that was shifting and churning like a great, awakening beast.

It was the pyramid itself, the whole colossal structure, turning on an axis that defied comprehension, its capstone splitting open like the petals of a great, stone flower to reveal a blinding iridescence that seared the eyes and set the mind reeling.

Deep beneath the earth, ancient passages that had slumbered for millennia began to stir. The same network of tunnels that honeycombed beneath Paris, beneath Rome, beneath the Congo Basin, beneath cities across every continent—the very networks Jarred had insisted were real—all led here, to this moment, this awakening. The pyramid wasn't just rising; it was drawing up the very arteries of the earth itself, pulling the scattered pieces of an ancient design back into alignment.

In that moment, as the world tilted on its foundations and the very fabric of reality seemed to warp and twist around them, Abbott Bruner knew with a certainty that transcended mere belief that everything he had ever known, every scrap of knowledge and wisdom he had accumulated over a lifetime of study and exploration, was but a mote of dust in the face of the truth that now stood before him, resplendent and terrible in its majesty.

The Great Pyramid, the towering enigma that had guarded its secrets for untold millennia, was awakening. And with its stirring, the world would never be the same again.

XXV. THE OPENING

Father Time adjusts the magiscope one final time, his ancient hands surprisingly gentle on the controls. Mother Earth leans against his shoulder, both of them watching with the intensity of parents at a graduation.

"Look at them," Mother Earth whispers, her voice thick with emotion. "After all this time, after all the separation and scattered languages... they're about to undo everything we did at Babel."

Father Time nods slowly, his expression thoughtful. "The tower rises again. But perhaps..." He pauses, considering. "Perhaps they've learned enough. Perhaps they've been without magic long enough to handle it responsibly this time."

"And if they haven't?" Mother Earth asks.

Father Time's weathered face breaks into a small smile. "Then we'll be here to clean up the mess. We always are."

They settle back to watch as Jesse steps toward destiny.

I stood across from Evelyn, transfixed by the swirling kaleidoscope of colors that danced before us, mesmerizing vortexes of light and energy that seemed to pulse in time with the beating of our hearts. In that moment, all the fear and uncertainty that had plagued us, all the doubts and questions that had haunted our every step, melted away like mist before the sun. Here, in the heart of the dolmen, with the amulets singing their siren song and the weight of destiny pressing down upon us, there was no room for anything but wonder, for the pure, awe that comes from standing on the brink of something greater than ourselves.

Evelyn's hand reached out, her fingers lacing with mine beneath the shimmering portals of light. Her touch was electric, a current of energy that raced up my arm and set my nerves ablaze. "I think, my love," she whispered, her voice soft and tremulous, "that I had found the man of the Earth a long time ago. I could have known, it was you all along."

My heart swelled with emotion, with a love so fierce and profound that it stole my breath. I reached with the amulet, my fingers around the woven cord, and lifted it reverently to the altar. "And I, Evelyn," I murmured, my gaze locked with hers, "have found my heavenly angel."

The miniature aurora borealis above the stone figures' hands seemed to reach out to us, caressing the surface of our amulets with gossamer fingers as we lowered them into place.

The cold of the metal reached up to my skin, thrumming with an ancient power that set my blood to singing. As the amulet settled into the waiting cradle of the hologram, the edges of the world seemed to blur and shift, reality bending around us like a lens warped by heat.

I leaned in, my lips finding Evelyn's in a kiss that seared my soul, that burned away the last vestiges of doubt and fear. In that moment, we were one, bound together by a love that transcended time and space, that defied the very laws of the universe.

As we parted, the amulets came together.

The stone figures began to move, their fingers closing around the amulets with a fluid grace that belied their rigid, inanimate nature. They lifted the pendants from their resting places, the pewter singing a high, clear note that seemed to vibrate in the very marrow of my bones. With a deft twist of their torsos, they raised their stone arms and took the amulets in agile fingers. The sun and moon spun apart like binary stars, opposing magnets afraid to touch. Between them in the cupped hands of the statues, a holographic image of the Earth formed.

Evelyn and I stumbled back, our eyes wide with wonder and trepidation as the figures began to rise, their stone limbs moving with a surreal, mechanical precision. It was as if they were marionettes, their strings pulled by some unseen hand, their movements guided by a will that was not their own. As they ascended, the slab beneath their feet tilted and shifted, the light from the tree trunk seeming to buoy them up, to lift them like corks bobbing on the surface of a rising tide.

The statues dropped their hands and the glowing earth hovered there. My gaze was trained on the eyes which seemed full of stars as the light drained away from the tree behind.

Then, for a moment, the chamber was plunged into darkness, a velvet blackness that pressed against my eyes like a physical weight. A second after pondering the last speck of light draining away, the eyes of the male figure began to glow, twin orbs of incandescent brightness, first slow, then in an instantaneous bolt of pure, unbridled power, the gaze went lancing through my skull.

I was transfixed, my gaze locked with the statue's, unable to look away even as the light grew to a blinding intensity. It was as if the figure was speaking to me, imparting some ancient wisdom, some secret knowledge that lurked just beyond the edges of my comprehension. I strained to hear, to understand, but the words were lost in the roar of blood in my ears, in the thundering of my own heartbeat.

Then I understood. I was a man who is, who was, and would be again. I saw the future and I saw the past. The design of the whole structure of time existed inside of the chamber and in the moment beaming into my retinas. I saw continents drifting apart like scattered children, then rushing back together in a cosmic embrace. I saw the great pyramid buried beneath sand and time, then rising like a phoenix to reclaim its place at the center of all things. I saw humanity scattered across the globe by divine will, and now, through love and choice, finding their way back to unity.

In that blazing instant of revelation, I understood that what Evelyn and I had done was not just personal destiny, but cosmic necessity—the healing of an ancient wound, the mending of a broken world.

Distantly, I heard Evelyn cry out, her voice high and sharp with fear. I tried to turn, to tear my gaze away from the mesmerizing light, but my body refused to obey, my muscles locked in a rictus of paralysis. In the peripherals I imagined the woman's figure close its eyes, the emerald radiance that had lined its face fading to a dull, lifeless grey.

And then the darkness claimed me, a vast, yawning void that swallowed me whole. I fell into it willingly, surrendering to the blissful oblivion of unconsciousness, my last coherent thought a fleeting, ephemeral thing that slipped through my grasp like smoke on the wind.

Evelyn. My love. My heart.

Remember...

XXVI. THE RISING

Mother Earth sighs as the waves surge. "More flooding?"

Father Time grins. "Not flooding, dear. Renewal. You of all people know water can cleanse and create. Magic is coming back to the world—look how beautifully it flows."

And, in the magiscope, those waters did indeed flow…

Along the eastern skyline of Peru, colossal mountains of water reared up like primordial beasts, their foaming crests reaching towards the heavens as the continent heaved and buckled. The ground shuddered and quaked, the tremors radiating outward in ever-widening ripples, as if the planet itself was a pond disturbed by a cast stone.

Across the globe, seaside cities found themselves battered and broken by the relentless onslaught of the rising tides. Skyscrapers that had once stood as gleaming testaments to human ingenuity crumpled like paper towers, their foundations undermined by the churning waters that surged through the streets like ravenous beasts. Bridges snapped and highways crumbled, the infrastructure of civilization reduced to rubble and ruin in the space of a heartbeat.

In Central America, the narrow band of land that had once connected the two great continents began to fracture and split, the earth itself torn asunder by the titanic forces at play. Residents of Costa Rica and El Salvador fled in panic, their homes and livelihoods devoured by the yawning chasms that opened up beneath their feet. The air was filled with the sound of screams and the thunder of collapsing buildings, a symphony of destruction that drowned out all other noise.

And at the heart of it all, rising from the depths like a colossus from myth, stood the Great Pyramid, its ancient stones shaking off the dust of ages as it ascended towards the sky. The capstones, those enigmatic blocks that had guarded the pyramid's secrets for millennia, began to slide back, revealing a blinding radiance that seared the eyes and set the mind reeling. It was as if the pyramid was awakening, stirring from a slumber that had lasted since the dawn of time itself.

Deep within the Earth's core, at the very center of the planet's molten heart, the Great Pyramid's base pulsed with an otherworldly energy, a force that sent shockwaves rippling outward through the surrounding rock and magma. It was here, in this crucible of primal creation, that the pyramid's true purpose was revealed, its connection to the Earth Mother herself laid bare for all to see.

Like a great, cosmic drawstring, the pyramid began to pull the scattered continents back towards itself, the landmasses moving ponderously across the surface of the planet like pieces on a chessboard. Mountains crumbled and valleys were rent asunder, the very geography of the Earth reshaped and redrawn in the blink of an eye. The seas boiled and churned, great whirlpools forming as the waters were dragged along in the wake of the shifting continents.

Chaos reigned supreme as the electromagnetic pulse generated by the polar shift swept across the globe, a silent, invisible wave of destruction that left devastation in its wake. Power stations erupted in showers of sparks and flames, their turbines and generators reduced to molten slag by the overwhelming surge of energy. Military installations, those bastions of human might and ingenuity, crumpled like tin cans, their weapons and vehicles rendered useless by the all-consuming pulse.

In the skies above, planes tumbled from the heavens like stricken birds, their engines choked and their instruments fried by the electromagnetic onslaught. They plummeted to the ground in streaks of fire and smoke, their passengers and crew consumed by the all-devouring flames. The air itself seemed to shimmer and warp, as if the very fabric of reality was being distorted by the cataclysmic forces at play.

On the land, animals of every kind fled in blind panic, their instincts screaming at them to seek higher ground, to escape the impending doom that loomed on the horizon. Herds of elephants and prides of lions, flocks of birds and swarms of insects, all moved as one, driven by a primal imperative that transcended the boundaries of species and kind. They surged towards the center of the newly-formed supercontinent, a great, teeming mass of life that sought to outrace the rising waters and the raging winds.

For the oceans themselves had become a devouring maw, great tsunamis racing towards the shores of Africa like the teeth of some immense, primordial beast. The waves towered over the land, their crests frothing and seething with an almost sentient rage, as if the Earth Mother herself was rising up to reclaim what was rightfully hers. The waters crashed against the shoreline with a force that shattered stone and rent metal, obliterating everything in their path with a casual, almost contemptuous ease.

Entire countries were swallowed up in the space of a heartbeat, their lands and peoples consumed by the relentless advance of the tides. Egypt, Sudan, Libya, Saudi Arabia - names that had once held such weight and meaning - were reduced to little more than memories, their cities and monuments swept away like grains of sand before the inexorable march of the waves.

And still the pyramid rose, a great, twisting spire that seemed to pierce the very heavens themselves. From space, it appeared as if a vast, inverted cyclone had taken hold of the Earth, the pyramid at its center drawing the landmasses towards it like iron filings to a lodestone. The continents collided with a force that shook the planet to its core, their edges crumpling and folding like the petals of some immense, geological flower.

At the boundaries of these newly-formed landmasses, where the earth met the sea, great jets of water erupted skyward, propelled by the unimaginable pressure generated by the convergence of the continents. The geysers rose to impossible heights, their columns twisting and writhing like the limbs of some gargantuan, aquatic beast. They hung suspended for a moment, defying gravity and reason alike, before crashing back down to the surface with a force that could shatter mountains and level cities.

And then, as suddenly as it had begun, the cataclysm was over. The pyramid stood tall and proud, its capstone brushing against the vault of the heavens, its surface gleaming with an otherworldly light. The waters that had once drowned the world began to recede, flowing back into the seas and oceans that now encircled the single, vast continent that had been birthed in the crucible of the Earth's transformation.

A great mist rose from the land and sea alike, a shimmering veil that hung in the air like a shroud of gossamer and lace. The sun, rising from the horizon like a phoenix from the ashes, cast its rays across this newly-formed world, the light refracting and splitting through the billowing fog in a dazzling display of color and radiance.

And there, hanging in the sky like a promise and a benediction, was a rainbow of such breathtaking beauty and scale that it seemed to encompass the entire Earth itself. Its colors were more vivid, more intense than anything that had ever been seen before, as if the primal forces that had reshaped the world had imbued the very air with a new and wondrous vitality.

To the East, the waves still crashed against the rocky shores of Eurasia, their thunder a distant echo of the cataclysm that had birthed this brave new world. And to the West, the gentler tides lapped against the pristine sands of Pangea.

XXVII. THE GARDEN

Evelyn cradled Jesse in her arms as the chamber shuddered and shifted, the walls groaning under the immense forces that swirled around them. High above, the opening to the world beyond had become a blinding portal of pure, radiant light, the brilliance slowly resolving into a tiny window of vivid blue sky. The air thrummed with the grinding of rock against rock, the very bones of the earth crying out as the great monolith twisted in its titanic ascent.

Even in the depths of the pyramid's heart, Evelyn could feel the world changing, could sense the reshaping of continents and the heaving of oceans through the miles of solid stone. The chamber bucked and swayed like a ship in a storm, and she held Jesse tighter, her heart hammering with fear and wonder as the very fabric of reality shifted around them. The grinding, rumbling cacophony grew to a deafening crescendo, then gradually began to fade, the violent shaking settling into gentle tremors, then finally, blessed stillness.

Exhaustion crashed over her like a wave. The terror, the cosmic forces, the sheer magnitude of what they had witnessed—it all pressed down upon her consciousness until she could no longer keep her eyes open. Still cradling Jesse protectively in her arms, Evelyn surrendered to the overwhelming fatigue and drifted into deep, dreamless sleep.

When she stirred, the quality of light had changed entirely. Soft, golden radiance filled the chamber, and the air carried new scents—flowers, earth, growing things. Jesse stirred beside her, both of them awakening naturally from their shared slumber.

The space around them had transformed. Where once solid stone had enclosed them, a passage now opened like a doorway carved from light itself. Warm, inviting brightness spilled through the opening, carrying with it the sweet scent of flowers and the distant sound of flowing water. The air itself seemed alive, tinged with moisture and the promise of new life.

The eternal statues remained, their stone forms still locked in that timeless embrace beneath the emerald tree, but something new had joined them. A brilliant scarlet macaw landed with a flutter of wings upon the male figure's outstretched arm, its feathers catching the strange new light. In its curved beak, it carried a single sprig of familiar blue-petaled flowers—Oxychana leaves, fresh and vibrant.

Evelyn's breath caught. The sacred plant of her people, here in this transformed space. The bird cocked its head at her, as if delivering a message from the Earth Mother herself: Your heritage lives on. Your roots can grow in new soil.

Jesse rose silently beside her, his movements careful and wondering. His beautiful blue eyes took in the bird, the passage, the light, but he spoke no words. Something profound had changed in him during that cosmic vision—not broken, but transformed, his memories scattered like seeds waiting to take root in fresh earth.

The macaw released the Oxychana sprig, letting it flutter to the mirrored floor between them, then spread its wings and soared through the passage toward whatever paradise lay beyond.

Evelyn took Jesse's hand, feeling his fingers close trustingly around hers. Together, they stepped toward the light, their bare feet finding the first of the basalt steps that led down through the passage. The walls around them glowed with their own inner radiance, quartz veins pulsing gently as they descended.

With each step, the air grew sweeter, the light brighter. Steam rose around them like incense, and ahead, through the widening passage, Evelyn caught glimpses of impossible green—leaves and vines and flowers beyond imagining.

They emerged into a world transformed, a land of breathtaking beauty and primal majesty. The air was sweet with the scent of morning dew, the moisture refracting the sun's rays into a shimmering veil of color that danced across the verdant landscape. A toucan called from the branches of a sprawling guava tree, its mate alighting beside it in a flutter of brilliant plumage.

Evelyn eased Jesse down onto a patch of soft grass, his back resting against the sun-warmed stone of the pyramid's base. She drank in the sight of him, marveling at the play of light across the planes of his face, the steady rise and fall of his chest. With a final, gentle touch, she turned and ventured out into the heart of the glade, her feet sinking into the rich, loamy soil.

The pyramid towered above her, its peak lost in the wispy clouds that drifted across the vault of the sky. It was a sight of such breathtaking scale and grandeur that Evelyn felt tears prick at the corners of her eyes, a lump forming in her throat as she tried to comprehend the miracle that had brought them to this place.

Beyond the lush foliage that dotted the glade, a snow-capped volcano loomed in the distance, its slopes wreathed in coils of steam that rose from its caldera like offerings to the heavens. Memories of her dream-flight with her mother, their hands entwined as they soared around the mountain's flanks, flashed through Evelyn's mind, a poignant reminder of the journey that had led her to this moment.

All around her, life flourished in riotous abundance. Flocks of birds wheeled overhead, their wings painting the sky in a kaleidoscope of color. A white-spotted fawn grazed at the edge of a tranquil pond, dappled sunlight playing across its coat as it nibbled at the tender shoots of huckleberry. In the sheltering embrace of a banyan tree, a jaguar lounged on a gnarled branch, its tawny fur rippling with each languid stretch.

In the chamber they'd left behind, the stone lovers remained locked in their eternal embrace, the emerald tree that arched over them drinking in the light that poured through the opening in the pyramid's peak. It was as if the heavens themselves had aligned to bless this sacred place, to bathe it in a radiance that transcended the boundaries of the mortal world.

As Evelyn explored the wonders of the glade, her gaze was drawn to a massive stone that jutted from the earth like a sentinel. Its surface was adorned with an intricate glyph, a stylized cross with arms of gold and silver that curved in perfect symmetry. A circle of purest light embraced the cross, the symbol of unity and balance that lay at the heart of creation.

Beneath the glyph, words had been carved into the stone, their lines as clean and precise as if shaped by a master's hand. "What is bred in the bone," Evelyn read, her voice a reverent whisper, "will not come out of the flesh."

And there, sprouting from the very base of the stone, were the unmistakable leaves of the Oxychana plant, the sacred herb that had played such a pivotal role in her own journey of self-discovery. She wondered for a moment if she might wake.

The glade was a paradise of unimaginable bounty, a cornucopia of fruits and flowers that seemed to pulse with the very essence of life. Apples of crisp red and burnished gold hung heavy from the boughs of ancient trees. Kiwis nestled in the embrace of their fuzzy skins, their tart sweetness a burst of flavor on the tongue. Cherries gleamed like rubies in the dappled sunlight, while vines heavy with ripe cantaloupes twined through the emerald grass.

Never in all her life had Evelyn felt such a profound sense of peace, of belonging. It was as if the very earth itself had reached out to cradle her, to whisper words of comfort and reassurance in her ear. Tears of joy streamed down her cheeks as she drank in the beauty that surrounded her, the sheer, overwhelming miracle of it all.

As she turned back to where Jesse lounged, Evelyn was struck by a sudden realization, a truth that burned bright and clear in her heart. They had been given a gift, she and Jesse, a chance to start anew in a world untouched by the sins and sorrows of the past. The knowledge and wisdom they had gained on their long, arduous journey would guide them now, would light the way forward as they built a life together in this place of wonder and promise.

Jesse stirred then, the gentle caress of a zephyr dancing across his grass-stained trousers and sandal-clad feet. He was at peace, a man awakening from one dream realm to the next, some recess of mind freed from past woes. His soulful blue eyes widened with a more conscious intelligence to behold a world of vivid colors and ethereal beauty - the swaying leaves glistening with fresh dew, flowers blooming in riotous hues, and exotic birds alighting on bountiful fruit trees.

He still said nothing, just marveled quietly as he rose, breathing in the sweet-scented air. The azure jaguar leapt gracefully into the boughs overhead while a peacock peeked coyly from behind broad ferns. He reached up to pluck a sun-ripened guava, relishing the tender fruit's nectar as it dribbled down his chin, the nearby birds unfazed by his presence.

But then he saw her, an exquisite woman adorned in naught but shells and sacred oil of color painted on her convex tummy, advancing slowly in his direction. The guava fell forgotten as he stood entranced by her radiance and poise, framed in a gilded shaft of light descending from a break in the clouds above.

"My love, welcome to our Eden," she said softly, reaching to press his hand tenderly against her heart. His mind quieted then, thoughts receding like the evening tide as he lost himself in her fathomless gaze and honeyed words.

Questions tugged at his awareness, voiced aloud as she nestled against his shoulder to admire the ring of stately trees and distant volcanic peak:

"Who am I?"

A warm smile played upon her lips as she replied, "Why you are my Adam, of course." Her gaze turned skywards as she continued, "And I..." But her voice trailed off, replaced by a whisper only her heart could hear:

"Eve."

And the trees awoke and knew them,
and the wild things gathered to them,
as they kissed amongst the wooded glen,
love growing manifold.

Deep within her womb, a child dreamed of riding horseback along the shores of a strange new world, rocking back and forth to the gentle sounds of a galloping heartbeat...

Epilogue: Mother Earth Speaks

She settles back in her cosmic La-Z-Boy, cocoa mug in hand, her expression growing distant and profound.

It was when he hovered over the surface of the deep that my curiosity began—and oh, was I curious. From my own waters did I create the fire that would drive the engine of creation and allow myself to experience my own magnificence. But in my vanity—and honey, was I vain—there was a flaw. That every single piece of life that was myself, formed on the same principles from whence I came, would possess the same curiosity of their origin that drove me within to seek it, I could not have known.

It was in the first bite of the forbidden fruit that threw the peace into turmoil. I should have seen the flaw, but I didn't. *Sigh.* On and on my people pressed and grew in worship, grasping at any belief or deity in hopes of finding natural balance once again. But even when every man came together with a single purpose and voice, it was not to enjoy more fully the unlimited life and knowledge they possessed, but rather to acquire more knowledge—which, hello, none existed.

A million years they built, with the unlimited power granted them by an unimaginably unlimited God. The very stones, which were bones of the earth, and soil my flesh, could be moved with the slightest effort. For faith was not lacking in the New World. Mountains were hewn and unhewn with nothing more than prayer. But even this boundless freedom they possessed couldn't push the single splinter from their minds as a people. The need for more was a thing I had birthed deep within each of my children, and was something I could not easily temper from them. *Talk about unintended consequences.*

It was not until the tower was completed from my own flesh and bone, created to draw down the light of the creator and imbue a watcher with its ultimate knowledge, that I begged the father to act. This single act of devastation to our own bodies of creation was a necessary experience to the growth process—harsh but fair, as he likes to say. Giving man in all of his glory the full understanding of his power was far too dangerous to do in a single instant. Becoming aware is a thing that takes millennia to achieve. The father and I have patiently waited through the enduring processes time and time again, but this we did on our own.

Man was different, for he came forth in abundance, and the brilliant minds of spiritual children were blind to the miracle of what they had already come to achieve with but minimum effort on their own part. Because the child feels as if they played no role in their own amazing creation—typical, really—they will seek to do and to know more, unconscious to the fact that they have already helped make miracles. It was only through time that we could allow our offspring the ultimate realization that creation is a triune process. As the three rays shine from the sun, so do the three elements imbue one another with the gift of life.

The Father's Love, the Mother's Body, and the Child's Will. Just as moon reflects the sun upon the earth, this triune is also apparent in the seasons of birth, life, and death. One grants power to another, it is a cycle, and an upward climb, which we have been hiking in an eternal journey for the plateau atop that beckons us.

In his own ignorance did early man seek out the thing he already owned and most coveted; yet he simply did not take responsibility for its possession. And so in a grand effort the Father cast the heavenly temple down into the center of the once unified land of man, segregating the continents and the languages, abashing his wasted efforts to gain knowledge of the unknown. True knowledge comes from within, and to tap it one need only know oneself. Complete universal knowledge, granted to a person from an outside source, would only cause total memory loss, for they would expect every answer to exist beyond their eternal reach, and their life would become a constant question.

As the Earth Mother, I am with my children along every step of the way and experience fully the emotion and growth of the people. But the Heavenly Father reminds us in our actions, on a daily basis, that the miracle of life that we have worked countless eons to create has not come about to ask the question,

"How did *I* come to be?"

But rather to question in the spirit and amazement of an innocent child,

"Now that we have achieved this amazing miracle, what together, shall we do next!?"

She takes a sip of cocoa and grins. And that, my dears, is parenting on a cosmic scale.

The Father Speaks

Father Time leans forward, beer in hand, his ancient eyes twinkling with both wisdom and mild exasperation.

It is the general way of things—ebb and flow, in and out, up and down, back and forth, right to left, black and white, good and bad, and on and on—these are the opposites. You get the idea. Too many times have I looked upon my reflection as I hovered over the surface of the deep, and expected that image to make me change. Millennia passed before it would ever slightly move my hand—*talk about taking your time*—and this was only after I had let the image looking back at me grow old and tired. Was youth my motivation to go within and seek more for myself?

Perhaps. Who knows? Even eternity doesn't guarantee understanding.

But in the end, it was I who called upon the beginning by reflecting on what I had experienced. It was I that questioned my past memories. It was I that faltered, and it was I that rose again. It was I who was fluent before being gifted with speech. It was I who was a drop in the air. It was I who was set adrift on a boundless sea, and it was I that grew for nine months in the womb.

It was I that kindled fire in the head. It was I that singly built the tower of Babel. It was I that doubted, and had forgotten, calling upon myself the darkness.

Yes, and I say that it was I that saw myself from the reflection of the mirror and only vaguely found the image familiar. And it was I that lived to experience every corner of emotion, from happiness to greed and back to loss and regret.

It was I who questioned them. It was I who sought an answer to why it was that they'd forsaken me. And it was I who'd forgotten the face of my father.

But in the end, when the brooding darkness enveloped me, I would see again his face. For the one thing I had left to gain was the one thing I had made for getting by forgetting it—my magnificence. And it was in this hour that the Father cried out from within,

"It is you!"

And finally it was I who dared to hear, and realize, that it was always me. And it was I who found myself asking myself back again:

"Who but I can let known the secrets of the unhewn dolmen?"

"Who but I can know the mystery of the moon?"

"Who but I can find the secret resting place of the sun?"

And finally,

"Who but I can now decide where this life will take me?"

Who but I?

Who but you?

HUBUDI

He raises his beer in a toast to the cosmic TV screen. And that, folks, is how you learn that being God is basically one long existential crisis with great special effects.

THE END

ENJOY THESE OTHER WORKS BY THE AUTHOR:

Chilling tales blend nostalgic Americana backdrops with doses of creepy whimsy à la Ray Bradbury. Wickedly humorous at times, make no mistake – malice lurks behind the smirks. Like classic Twilight Zone, these stories shock more than they soothe.

The Death of Science is a twisted and humorous foray into the vast multi-faceted universe of Rootworld. Like a contemporary Twilight Zone, this satirical science fiction fantasy tale will appeal to fans of both the nostalgic familiar as well as the shockingly bizarre.

The Tome of Ages is the second installment in the Rootworld Series. Hazeus, gets crucified and returns home to Father Time and Mother Earth where he is forced to watch the adult-rated MVD's his parents have been keeping until he's come of age.
He finds out, in no small trials, that becoming the God Zeus will not be without some Earthly meddling in the affairs of King Arthur and Merddin, his tutor.
Return to familiar characters across genres and escape into the magical realm of Rootworld.

Perfect for bedtime reading, this charming children's adventure follows a bugs-eye view of the animal kingdom as a plucky band of fleas and lice seek to establish their own empire. Echoing the whimsical imaginings of Terry Pratchett's The Carpet People, these tiny explorers face giant obstacles with camaraderie and wit. Young readers will delight in accompanying the brave King Fleo and quick-thinking Queen Clouse on a quest filled with thrills as they traverse the wild frontiers of fur and skin. This amusing bedtime tale brings the miniature world of animals and bugs to vivid life.

Children's/ Bedtime/ Adventure/ 40 Minute Read

Doctor Datson is getting older, but that doesn't keep him from still getting into mischief.
When one of his lab experiments re-animates some old fossils, it is up to Truman and the rest of the gang to track down the dangerous creatures and find out who's responsible.
30 Minute Flash Fiction
Science Fiction/Thriller/Humor

Also by Jay Horne:

The Death of Science: A Novel Introduction to Rootworld

A Project Gone Bad: Terror at Lowry Park Zoo

O-zone

Appassionata in F-Minor

Fossil Fuel

Still Perfect

The Groundsman

Twit's Do It Better

A Brumby's Best Friend

A Lousy Bedtime Story

Lawn Chair

Dingo Dango

A Last Tribe's First Christmas

Boiler Room

www.ingramcontent.com/pod-product-compliance
Lightning Source LLC
Chambersburg PA
CBHW070838020826
48982CB00021B/1473/J

* 9 7 9 8 9 9 1 3 8 3 1 0 3 *